The Sound of Holding
Your Breath

NO LONGER PROPERTY OF
SEATTLE PUBLIC LIBRARY

The Sound of Holding Your Breath

STORIES

NATALIE SYPOLT

WEST VIRGINIA UNIVERSITY PRESS • MORGANTOWN 2018

Copyright © 2018 by Natalie Sypolt
All rights reserved
First edition published 2018 by West Virginia University Press
Printed in the United States of America

ISBN:
Paper 978-1-946684-57-8
Ebook 978-1-946684-58-5

Library of Congress Cataloging-in-Publication Data
Names: Sypolt, Natalie.
Title: The sound of holding your breath : stories / Natalie Sypolt.
Description: First edition. | Morgantown : West Virginia University Press, 2018.
Identifiers: LCCN 2018011389 | ISBN 9781946684578 (pb)
Classification: LCC PS3619.Y925 A6 2018 | DDC 813/.6--dc23
LC record available at https://lccn.loc.gov/2018011389

Book and cover design by Than Saffel / WVU Press

Stories from this collection have appeared in the following publications:
"At the Lake," *Slippery Elm*, Summer 2016; "Diving," *Kenyon Review Online*, Volume IV, no. 1, Winter 2011; "Flaming Jesus," *Potomac Review*, Fall 2005; "Home Visit," *Still: The Journal*, Issue 7, Fall 2011; "Love, Off to the Side," *Still: The Journal*, Issue 4, Fall 2010; "My Brothers and Me," *Glimmer Train*, Winter 2013; "Lettuce," *Willow Springs Review*, Issue 67, Spring 2011; "Handlers," *Kestrel*, Issue 21, 2007; "What Would Be Saved," *Queen City Review*, Fall 2009; "The Sound of Holding Your Breath," *Still: The Journal*, Issue 22, Fall 2016; "Stalking the White Deer," *Appalachian Heritage*, Spring 2015.

C. D. Wright, excerpt from "Everything Good Between Men and Women" from *Steal Away: Selected and New Poems*. Copyright © 1996, 2002 by C. D. Wright. Reprinted with the permission of The Permissions Company, Inc. on behalf of Copper Canyon Press, www. coppercanyonpress.org.

For Mom and Dad

———

For Ma and Pappy

The first few tongues are clearly
preparatory. The impression
made by yours I carry to my grave. It is
just so sad so creepy so beautiful.
Bless it. We have so little time
to learn, so much. . . . The river
courses dirty and deep. Cover the lettuce.
Call it a night. O soul. Flow on. Instead.

—C. D. Wright,
from "Everything Good Between
Men and Women"

Contents

Diving

---

 oday is Thanksgiving and Maggie and Mom are peeling potatoes. They cube and drop them into a pan of murky water that sits between them on the table. Mom's potatoes are smooth and white. Maggie's are chopped and little specks of brown cling to them even after they fall into the water. I stand in the doorway, just there listening and waiting for something to happen. I'd felt a secret coming, felt it in the air like some people feel snow, and I knew it wasn't in the front room with Daddy and Uncle Jimmy or out back with my brothers.

"John Simpson," Mom says and I nearly lose my lean on the wall. She doesn't look up at me, but keeps right on peeling, cubing, dropping. "What are you doing there?"

"Just thought I'd help," I say and see Maggie roll her eyes.

"I don't know why Dan Vee won't just quit." Maggie is back on the talk they'd been having before Mom saw me hanging at the door. "Can you imagine it, Mommy? Diving down there? Risking your own neck, just to find nothing but—God, I shiver to think of it."

"So they still haven't pulled it up?" Mom doesn't take her eyes off the knife. My face goes hot and I hold myself to the door to keep from moving.

"The river's too rough. You know how it gets around this time of year, and if it starts snowing, I don't know. Part of me wishes they'd just forget it and let them be."

"Poor Chad. Didn't you and Dan Vee go to school with him?"

I remember a sound bite from the TV news. All the local stations had fallen on Green River soon as the news broke. The baby's daddy had said, "I'm not moving from this riverbank until they bring him up and put him in my arms. Right here in my arms." The news people loved that and kept playing it, over and over in a loop. Every time you turn on the TV, "put him in my arms."

Some sixteen-year-old babysitter had been driving and made it out alive. The neighbor boy was still in the car. The girl said he could have got out, too, but wouldn't with the baby there, all crying and still strapped in.

"I don't know how to feel for that girl," Maggie says and more marred potato chunks go *plunk* into the water. Mom motions me to the table, but I can't move. "I guess I want to feel sorry for her, but it's hard."

"John Simpson," Mom says. "Come take this knife." Mom's chair makes a squeaking baby scream as it scratches the cracked tile floor. The sound pulls me to the table and pushes me into the warm seat.

Maggie wants to smoke. I can tell because she is chewing gum so fast that sometimes her teeth hit together.

I pick up Mom's knife and try not to press too hard.

"I suppose I should start on the noodles," Mom says.

"Noodles?" Maggie is at distraction, watching me cut and stab my poor potato. "Oh, who cares? Do you know Dan Vee's barely eaten since this all started? I make him dinner and he just stares at it, like it's something he don't understand."

"No one should have to see what he's seen, Maggie. You can't be so hard on him." Some mothers would come and hug their girl, but mine just stands there.

"He could've just kept on with the department, going in for fires and car wrecks, but he just had to do the extra training, just had to learn to be a diver."

"Dan Vee always has been a strong swimmer," I say and they both look at me like I'd just broken a glass. "He was on the swim team."

Maggie wants to say, "Don't talk, Johnny." That's what she would've said when we were both still kids.

I picture my sister's husband, high-school swim-team captain, pushing through lanes of water. I'd been just in the seventh grade when he'd graduated, but I remember standing, cheering him on, screaming louder even than Maggie. After, he'd come out of the locker room, his hair still wet and all of him smelling like water a hundred boys had sweated into. He'd come out and look so easy in his skin that I didn't know what else to do but turn around and run.

I'm in high school now but can't swim worth a damn.

My three brothers are all good at sports. Always playing football or deer hunting or driving beat-up pickup trucks. My oldest brother Danny drives to community college and Peter works for the Foodland. Caleb is a senior and I'm a junior, but at school we don't know each other. "Toughen up," they tell me. They hit me on the arm, hard but then laugh like it's a joke. Sometimes Mom tells them to leave me be, but mostly she just pretends not to see.

Dan Vee works for the county as an EMT and is real good at his job. I know because in September, I fell down a little bank walking home from school. I didn't so much fall as slide, and when I saw the hole in my jeans' knee and the scrape on my skin underneath, I did it again. Then I ran into a telephone pole, ran hard and wrapped so the wood hit my ribs in a way that made me lose my breath. It was like there was somebody there—one of those guys from school or one of my brothers—somebody hugging me then hitting me, kicking me when I was on the ground and rubbing my face into the dirt.

I lay on the ground, trying to catch my breath. When I could, I got up and walked. There I was at Maggie's door, leaning heavy against her porch railing because it was hard to breathe.

"Oh, good God," Maggie said when she opened the door and saw me, bloody and dirty. "What happened, Johnny?" Her hands fluttered over me like she was afraid to touch, and I tried to think something about her, something nice, but it was like my brain was all swelled up.

"Jesus H., John." I heard Dan Vee's voice from behind Maggie, and when I did, I pushed her away. I saw some look on her face, like hurt or surprise, maybe.

When Dan Vee took me downstairs, Maggie didn't follow us. He got out his kit full of white bandages and other stuff that smelled like hospital. Maggie and Dan Vee had one of those finished basements with wall-to-wall carpeting and an old sofa and some other little touches like a TV and a mini-refrigerator. Last year, Dan Vee put in a pool table and taught me how to play.

I tried not to wince as he cleaned my face, rinsed the blood, and said it wasn't as bad as it looked. My shirt front was wet from my nose bleeding. I felt ashamed over what I done, but some sickness had come over me for just that minute out on the road, something like a seizure that I couldn't help, and I didn't say a thing to Dan Vee.

Dan Vee helped me peel my shirt off, real gentle over my head and the pain from my side blew so hot white that I couldn't breathe.

"Let me see," he said and put his hands on me, pressing around my ribs, moving his thumbs slow. His motions were firm and sure and I felt like I could be any boy. Car accident. House fire.

"I don't think they're broke," he said. "But you best go in and get X-rays, just in case."

Maggie called him from the top of the stairs. Dan Vee squeezed my shoulder and told me to hold tight.

I could hear voices—Maggie's fast and high, Dan Vee's slower and even. Maggie had lots of questions, wanted to call my school or the cops, maybe. Dan Vee told her to let it be.

When he came back down, he threw me one of his T-shirts, dark blue and clean, so when I pulled it on, it smelled like soap and not like Dan Vee. I waited for him to say something, but he just pressed a Band-Aid over the cut in my eyebrow.

"Maggie's gonna drive you home," he said, looking me right in the eye. "You call if you need to or if your pain gets worse. Okay, John?" He didn't ask what happened, but he never did tell me to leave when I started coming over most days after school.

———————

"I suppose it sounds selfish, me wanting him just to quit, but I don't care. We'll have this baby soon and who knows what kind of daddy he'll make after seeing all these dark things?" Maggie rubs her hand in a circular motion over her big belly. It's the hand with the knife and I watch the little silver blade press on the fabric of her shirt, tight fitted over her and Dan Vee's baby. I wondered how that drowned baby's skin looked, what Dan Vee saw when he looked in those back windows. Maybe blue like on TV, or maybe the cold water, like ice, had kept him perfect. That might be even worse. If he looked alive, and Dan Vee's brain said "alive," but then when Dan Vee couldn't pull him out, he'd have to leave him there and that would be worse than seeing a dead blue baby.

"Where is Dan Vee?" I ask.

Maggie says, "Where do you think?"

I was there at the house a couple weeks ago, playing pool with Dan Vee when Maggie came home from work and started giving me shit. "Christ Johnny," she said. "Why are you over here so much? Don't you have any friends?" Dan Vee was sitting in a beat-up recliner, waiting on me to take my turn, and Maggie dumped herself down into his lap. The next thing I know, she's got her shirt pulled up over her belly and is telling Dan Vee to put his hand on her. "Right here," she was saying and pressing his hand to her stretched white skin. I watched as his big hand found the place, the sweet spot where the baby's foot jabbed at Maggie's insides. I remembered the cat we'd had when I was little and how you could feel the kittens moving around inside her.

"You okay there, John? You look a little green," Dan Vee said. He and Maggie were both looking at me. Maggie rolled her eyes, but I thought I saw a smile at the edges of Dan Vee's mouth.

"I was just thinking of that old barn cat Sugar. You remember that one time when she had kittens in your underwear drawer, Maggie? God, what a mess."

"Go home why don't you?" Maggie pushed herself up and rolled her shirt back down over her round belly. I wondered if Dan Vee wanted to wash his hand.

I lined up my shot and watched as the cue ball went barreling into the side pocket like I'd meant it to do. "Scratch. Damn," I said. "Your turn, Dan Vee." Maggie stomped back up the stairs and slammed the door when she got to the top.

"Don't get me wrong, John. I love your sister," Dan Vee said. "But girls? They're nothing but trouble."

"Trouble," I said like I knew. I made up some story then without even thinking, about a girl at school named Bonnie, who didn't exist but still gave me nothing but trouble. Dan Vee laughed and gave me a beer out of the mini-fridge. I knew I shouldn't 'cause Mom would give me hell, but I took it anyway. Dan Vee clapped his big hand on the back of my neck, the same big hand that had touched Maggie, and told me I was "all right."

I'm still just on my first potato, worrying the knife around and around. It's getting real little, but I can't quite manage to get it clear. "I can take Dan Vee over some dinner," I say.

"You'd like that, wouldn't you?" Maggie says, voice full of hatefulness.

"That'd be nice," Mom says, like she hasn't heard Maggie at all.

"Maybe I shouldn't even have come," Maggie says. "He probably shouldn't even be left alone. You don't know, Mommy, you just don't know. I didn't want to say it, but I heard him crying last night. He thought I was asleep, but I wasn't. I felt the bed shake." This is what she's been holding in, all along.

Mom asks her, "Well, what did you do?"

"I know how they all say it's okay for them to cry, but he's never in all the years I've known him. I just kept pretending to be asleep." Mom doesn't say anything but nods a little and I know that's what she would've done too.

I hate my sister for pretending to be asleep while Dan Vee lay there, so alone with that dead baby face in his head.

I picture myself getting up from that table, pushing back my chair and dropping the potato knife. Maggie and Mom would both look at me like they don't understand. I'd go out the back door and walk to Dan Vee's. When I got there, my face would be freezing and red. I'd almost not be able to feel my fingers when I pounded on the door. Or I wouldn't pound. I'd just go in and find Dan Vee in the basement. He'd be down there playing pool or watching football. Or maybe he'd be there with his head in his hands, with his shoulders shaking and noises like a baby makes coming up from him. What I saw myself do next was what didn't fit, what I didn't know how to see. Me wiping Dan Vee's tears. Putting them on my own burning-red, frozen-red face. Dan Vee laying his big hands there to warm my cheeks, my nose, my mouth.

"Johnny!" Maggie screams.

She's looking at my hand, and then I see the slice down my palm, top to bottom like it's supposed to be there, like the lifeline or love line or fortune line. The cut is burning and running red. Mom comes at me with a dish towel and is saying to put my hand above my head, but I don't move. Blood drips into the pot, turning the potato water red. Ruined.

Flaming Jesus

———

This is a place where no one cares if you live in a trailer. No one even thinks twice about it. Often, the "mobile homes" that are really only mobile once in their lives, are nicer and safer than the little wooden houses, drafty and cold. All homes, trailers and wooden houses, are fire traps. Maybe that's how my hometown, which wasn't really a town, just residences randomly dotting a few dozen miles of West Virginia, got its name: Warm. Though fire is hot, seldom warm, the ashes that smolder are.

My mother always had wallpaper. We'd replace it every spring when it would start to peel. I remember the smell of the wallpaper paste and how she would stretch, up on her tiptoes, pressing her body against the wall and reaching to tuck the edges beneath the moldings. I lived in a trailer for most of my young life, before my grandfather died when I was fifteen and left us his run-down farm with rotten potatoes still in the ground. We lived in a single-wide, white and gray. I was never ashamed.

There is a long stretch of road with no houses. The roadsides are thickly wooded, branches nearly scraping my car on both sides. The very sunlight has a hard time coming through. Only the roadway is light, golden. I feel a pull as the land inclines. I know soon the hill will top out, the woods will break, and there will be a structure. I hold my breath as the way gets brighter, watch as, seemingly out of nowhere, the simple white church appears. There is one stained-glass window of the resurrected Messiah in the attic and only a plain sign outside that reads "Warm Church All Welcome."

My one teenage love was Josiah Mayhew, the stereotypical son of a preacher man from my youth. I had just turned fifteen. He was two years older, more sinner than saint. He scared me. Fear was a dangerous thing to mix with love. He'd sit in a front pew on Sunday, looking gloomy and wearing all black. Sometimes he'd pretend to sleep, sometimes draw in his Bible, anything to ignore his father as he pounded the pulpit with his left hand and held his right claw-like fist close to his side, slightly tucked under his robes. I never knew what had happened to his arm, but I did know this was the one that scared Josiah, deep down where he wouldn't admit. Though the fingers didn't work, the reverend would use his arm like a club, blasting the wickedness out of his deviant son. Most everyone in Warm knew a little about it but didn't think any less of Reverend Mayhew. It was Josiah who was bad, wrong, for making his daddy—such a good man—resort to those measures.

One bright and blazing August Sunday Josiah came to church with a purple bruise around his eye. I was watching the light from the window reflect on the shiny blackness of his hair when he turned around and looked at me. The bruise made his right eye look so blue while the other was the same, dark and clear. He looked magical. He smiled at me a little. His smile was crooked and he had a dimple in his right cheek.

After we moved to the farm, Josiah would come late at night and throw pebbles at my window until I climbed down the crooked quake ash that grew outside my room. It was close enough for him to walk from his perfect white house on Columbia Road, but still a fair distance and he was always red faced and flushed as he put his hands around my waist and helped me take the final step onto the ground.

We'd walk and he'd push his fingernails lightly into the palm of my hand. More often than not, we'd end up at Warm Church. He had a key because his father made him clean the pews and floor after Sunday services, but he always broke in by jimmying the lock on the back door. We wouldn't even stop downstairs, but would head straight for the closet in Reverend Mayhew's office. There was the pulldown staircase that led to the attic.

I call it an attic, but it wasn't really. It was just a tiny space, big enough only for someone to crawl up and clean the window or to reach the heavy rope that rang the bell for weddings or funerals.

He came so late one night in mid-September that I had already been asleep for hours, deep in a dream about my Uncle Saul who died in a farm accident when I was five. Uncle Saul had never left Warm, not even for a short time during the war, like some of the other town men, because of his bad eyesight. In my dream I saw him in Paris. A blonde French woman snapped his photo in front of the Eiffel Tower.

I don't know how long Josiah had thrown rocks at the side of the house before I finally woke up and came to the window. "Come down," he said huskily and I did, without even putting on shoes.

It was so dark I had to make my way down the tree by memory. As always, he helped me from the last branch and I could smell the musky scent of him. I'd never been able to decide if he wore cologne or just naturally smelled like oil and wood. He kissed me quick, on the side of the mouth, then pulled me through our yard and toward the woods.

I watched Josiah's hands shake as he worked the lock. An outside light was always left on at Warm Church, for the wayfaring stranger who could stop to pray outside but not cross the sacred threshold until Ms. Betty came at ten to unlock the door. Under that light, Josiah's skin looked clammy and yellow. I noticed his thick, dark hair was wet, falling thickly into his face. Finally, the door creaked open and we were inside and to the attic before I could blink.

We always went to the window. Josiah would sit against it and I would sit in front of him, our knees touching. Sometimes, when there was a bright moon, light would come through the window onto his face. I loved to watch as the different colors were projected on his nose and cheekbone. This night there was no moon.

"I'm leaving, Neva," he said finally, his first words since we'd left my house. I felt punched in the stomach, but not shocked. I'd known this day was coming. "Tonight. I'm going."

"I'm sorry," Josiah said. First, I thought he was apologizing for running away, for leaving me alone, but when I looked up at him, trying to find his eyes in the dark, I saw that he was staring down at my upturned hand. "I made your hand bleed. I'm sorry." I held my palm close to my eyes and saw four tiny red half-moons where his fingernails had broken my skin. "He wants to send me away to some religious reform school in godforsaken Kentucky, Neva. I can't go, and I can't stay." I felt tears start to well but ordered myself not to lose control. "Do you ever want to leave here? Do you ever want to just go?" he asked. I shrugged. While I thought about growing up, leaving home and doing things incredible and exotic, Warm always played a part. Even in my most fantastic daydreams, there was a feeling of home and family that I could never escape.

"Warm's not so bad." In my mind I had visions of harsh cities with skyscrapers that blocked out the stars, and people who looked down on us for happily living in trailers and never trying to "better our situations."

"It's a trap, Neva. This whole town, it's just a trap. If I don't get out now, I never will. Look around us. No one goes anywhere. To Myrtle Beach for the weekend? Screw that. Not me." He wanted to get up, to pace and rage. I could tell by the way he cracked his knuckles and nervously moved his feet around on the dusty floor. "Everyone acts like I owe them something. I'm supposed to be a good boy, go to church and keep up my old man's pretty reputation. Grow up and go to work in the mines or the sawmill, come home every day to Warm. Bullshit. To hell with doing what I'm supposed to do. I'm not staying here and being a martyr for this town or for my father or for anyone." I put my hand on his chest; the pain in my hand pulsing with the beat of his heart.

"I want to show you something." From his jacket pocket, Josiah pulled a tiny figure and a cheap lighter. He lit the lighter so I could see the object he held in the palm of his hand. It was a small plastic Jesus, an altar decoration I'd seen often downstairs along with the nativity. Jesus was robed in white, grieved face upturned and arms lifted toward heaven. "Watch." Slowly, Josiah moved the flame closer and closer to the Jesus; finally, the hot flame touched the base. The plastic began to melt. Something caught and the whole thing was on fire. Josiah let the lighter go out and dropped it next to him. I've never seen anything burn like that statue. Through the tiny, lapping flames, I watched it melt. I watched as the nose, the ethereal blue eyes, then the whole head dissolved. I looked from the burning Jesus to Josiah, to the flames reflecting in his eyes. The flames rose and consumed. It had to hurt. To burn him. I couldn't take it anymore. I hit his hand from underneath, making what was left of the flaming Jesus fall onto the floor. We watched it burn there for a second before Josiah stamped it out with his boot.

"He keeps buying the damn things," he said. I could feel the weight of his hand, upturned, lying on my knee. In the brief flash of light before the Jesus was extinguished, I'd seen the round burn in the center of his palm. "Every week I steal it and set it on fire, but he just keeps buying the damn things. Can't imagine anyone stealing Jesus. I think he believes it's a miracle or sign or something, the way they keep disappearing." For the first time I realized that I'd never really seen this place in the light of day. How long had he been burning

Jesus statues? I pictured charred bits and pieces of our savior lying all around me.

I kissed him once, expecting his lips to feel hot as fire, hot as the Jesus, but they were cold and emotionless. I wanted to say something, maybe "I love you," maybe "don't go," maybe something else, but I never got the chance.

"Go home, Neva." Josiah turned his back to me, facing the beautiful stained-glass window. The last I saw before backing down the tiny stairs was his figure, silhouetted against the bright panel as if his dark shape was meant to be there, part of the design.

Josiah left that night. I heard rumors that before he left, he opened a Bible on his dining-room table, put the last Jesus figure in the crease, and set it all on fire. The smoke detector went off and Reverend Mayhew rushed down to put it out before any real damage was done. No one but me really believed the whole story.

I couldn't trust my own memory. In the days after he left, it all became impossible. In my memory, the flames from the burning Jesus shot up, blue, green, orange. Josiah's eyes, too, burned when he looked at me. There was light in the attic—from the window, the fire, Josiah himself—but really I know it was dark. So dark that I only glimpsed the burn on his hand, but in my memory, that flash had lasted for hours. The burn seemed huge, raw and pulsating. Everything burned.

Reverend Mayhew searched passionately for Josiah and held prayer meetings for his safe return. I would go to Warm Church, hold hands, and pray as Revered Mayhew spoke through a lump in his throat about his misguided son. One week, I would fervently pray for Josiah to come home; the next week, I would pray just as hard that he would never have to set foot in Warm again.

Josiah was gone for eight months. I heard his father found him working on a fishing boat somewhere near the ocean. Reverend Mayhew claimed it was divine intervention—a miracle that returned his son to him.

The first time I saw Josiah after he came home, it was in church. He sat in his pew, slumped and wearing black, looking as if he had never left. I watched the back of Josiah's head, remembering the first time I'd seen the light from the window bounce off his hair like it was metal. I made a fist and with the tips of my fingers felt the half-moon-shaped scars in my palms.

Finally, Josiah turned toward me. His eyes were dull.

I wanted to talk to him, to ask about what he'd done, about what he'd seen; to find out what had beaten him. Was it the coming back or the going away?

While my mother wasn't looking, I took a pen from my purse, opened my Bible, and scribbled a hasty secret note across Revelations 9:1–9. "Josiah, meet me after church in our place. If I can get away, you can. Neva."

I ripped out the page as quietly as I could, balled it up, and held it in my hand until Reverend Mayhew decided it was time for the altar call. Never before had I made the trip from my seat, up the aisle, to let Reverend Mayhew pray over me, put his hands on my head, help me welcome Christ into my life.

Josiah was sitting on the end of the first pew. When Reverend Mayhew raised his arms and asked who among his lambs needed to approach the altar, I stood and silently made my way over my mother and to the aisle.

I felt every eye on me as I took careful steps toward Reverend Mayhew. Macey Goodyard was already up there, along with Harlen Miles, but they took altar call nearly every week. It was me the congregation watched. I held my head high and focused my eyes on the huge crucifix behind Reverend Mayhew's head.

I walked close to the pews, letting my arms dangle. I knew when I was next to Josiah, could feel it, could smell him. I seamlessly opened my hand and dropped my note into his lap. I took five more steps and hit my knees. I cringed when Reverend Mayhew's hands touched my hair and knelt deeper. My forehead was touching his floor; I bowed at his feet.

After everyone had filed out of the church, I told my mother I'd forgotten my purse and had to run back inside. It wasn't a lie. I had left it lying on our pew. It just hadn't been an accident.

I had never seen the tiny attic room in daylight, but I could still tell things were different. It was cleaner, dusted, less cluttered. I looked around on the floor for a burnt spot, the place where Josiah had stamped out the burning Jesus with his boot, but saw nothing.

I had been in the stuffy and hot space for ten minutes and didn't know how much longer I'd be able to wait. I was looking out the stained-glass window, thinking how different the view was from the inside, looking out on a colored, fragmented world, when I heard someone coming.

"I've only got a minute," Josiah said as he bent low to keep from hitting his head. "I told him I was going to the bathroom."

"This place looks different in the daylight, huh?" I said, feeling nervous. I couldn't look him in the eyes.

"I cleaned it up. Neva, what did you want? I've got to get back out there."

"I just wanted to talk to you. I wanted to know what happened. Where did you go? What was it like? Everything." Finally he sat down across from me, his knee touching mine, and I began to relax. I waited for him to say something—for his face to turn red and for the angry words to start again, but they didn't.

"Neva," he said softly, not looking at me but at his own hands. "You don't want to know everything."

"Yes I do! What was it like, Josiah? To be away from here?" He was quiet for a few beats then looked up at me.

"It wasn't any different. The way things looked changed, the people's faces, but for me, it all just stayed the same."

"What do you mean?"

15

"I thought that if I got out of here, everything would be so much better, but every place I went, it all just followed me. This place. My father. I kept hearing his voice in my head. I knew he was coming."

I reached out to touch his hand, but he pulled it away. "I've gotta go. The best thing you can do, forget about me."

"But what are you going to do?" I was crying and didn't try to hide it. He didn't seem to notice.

He didn't say goodbye. He just turned and went back downstairs, leaving me alone in the thick air.

When Reverend Mayhew announced Josiah's plans one day during Sunday services, everyone was proud. Josiah had waited out his days until he turned eighteen and joined the Navy. "He's leaving immediately," my mother told me when she came home. "Wants to be stationed somewhere overseas. He was a different boy after coming back. Like a whole new person. Getting a taste of the real world sure did change that one." No, it hadn't, I thought. He'd been polite. He'd gone to church and didn't disobey, but here he was, running again. It looked prettier than before. The town saw him as brave, as a patriot, but I knew the truth. He was just taking to the water this time, using the more traditional route of escape for small-town boys who didn't want to be.

Ghosts

But the ghosts that I got scared and I got high with look a little
lost . . . but those were different days.

—Jason Isbell, "Different Days"

I.

*T*he Golden Egg didn't do much business during lunchtime Mondays
through Fridays, better on the weekends, but dinnertime and later was
the only time they really made much money. It was quiet enough that
Joan could sit at one of the long tables and tally receipts and make
out the orders for the next week. Her daughter-in-law Courtney was
supposed to be waiting tables, but mostly just sat across from Joan,
cracking her gum and watching *Let's Make a Deal* on the big TV
over the bar.

"Look at that," she said as a grown, hairy man wearing a diaper and
holding a giant rattle stood next to the host, jumping up and down,

and waving an oversized pacifier in the air. "I would not embarrass myself on the TV like that for any amount of money."

"Hmmm," Joan said, but didn't say what she was thinking, which was that embarrassing yourself wasn't so bad if money was on the other end, not when money was what you needed. You'd get over being embarrassed. She figured Courtney never would really understand that, though, not growing up like she had in one of the neat little houses near town. Now her and Joan's son Marcus lived in one of those prefab deals that Marcus would be paying on for the rest of his life—and maybe sending checks from the other side too—but at least he knew what the other kind of life was like.

"If you were going on that show," Courtney said, "What would you go as?" Joan knew that this was one of those questions Courtney asked just so she could answer it herself. She didn't really care what Joan thought, so Joan just shrugged and punched some numbers into her noisy old adding machine. She'd lost all track of what she was doing but didn't want to encourage Courtney to talk anymore.

"Well, I believe I would be something like a naughty nurse, or maybe a naughty police officer," she said. "Something short and tight because then you'd be more likely to get on camera. And I tell you one damn thing—" The little bell over the door jingled as a man and woman, people Joan didn't recognize, came in. Courtney pushed herself up from the table. "I would never take that box, and I'd never give up what I got for some curtain. Screw the curtain."

Joan *hmmmm*-ed again. One reason Joan had asked Courtney to move from nighttime to the earlier shift was because it made her uncomfortable watching the girl married to her son lean low over tables full of men or throw her head back laughing like one of them had just said the funniest thing she'd ever heard. "It's just for tips," Marcus told Joan, but she wasn't so sure. Joan thought that Courtney'd probably take that mysterious curtain number one every time.

"Hey y'all!" Courtney said to the couple, then led them to a table near the bar. "What can I get you to drink?"

The man—a tall fellow wearing a faded Mountaineers ballcap and blue jeans—ordered a beer. The woman just wanted ice water with lemon. The way she said it—"just ice water with lemon"—made it clear that the water best be free and that they better not try to charge for the glass. Or the lemon.

"I'll just give you all a few minutes to decide what you might want to eat," Courtney said, sweet as honey dripping from the honeycomb. She rolled her eyes at Joan as she walked by on her way to the pop dispenser.

"Hey Granny!" Joan turned in her chair to see April, her fourteen-year-old granddaughter swinging out of the kitchen. She was wearing black leggings and a gray WPMS sweatshirt that barely covered her butt. Her long brown hair was in a high, thick ponytail.

"Well hey there girl," Joan said. April dropped down into the chair next to her, and Joan noticed that her eyes were outlined in black. Every time she saw the girl wearing makeup, her stomach clinched and she had to bite down hard on her tongue to keep from saying something. "What are you doing here? I thought you had some afterschool thing."

"Track practice," April said, pulling a few school books out of her bag and stacking them on the table next to Joan's piles of work. This was a ritual they'd had since April was little. The school bus would drop her off at The Egg and then they'd do their work side by side until her daddy'd come in and pick her up after work. "It was cancelled 'cause of the rain. Do you know it's supposed to snow, Granny? Can you believe it? I can't. It's April!"

"Oh, it ain't so unusual," Joan said. "My daddy said he's seen snow as high as a horse's belly in May."

"No thank you!" April said. "I am ready for the sunshine!"

"Me too, but I sure am glad that I get to see you today." Ever since she'd heard the news at noontime, she'd been wanting to see April, just to touch her hair and know her realness, her aliveness, for a minute. Those TVs blaring, always blaring away, and the news at noon came on without anybody really noticing it, until they started talking about Preston County, which they hardly ever did since nothing much happened there and no one outside of the county really cared about the little that did. There was a drowning, the anchor said. It'd happened late the night before or early that morning. A fifteen-year-old boy whose name was not being released. It'd been down at that bridge, the one where all the young people and the college kids from the neighboring county came to drink and get high and swim. Every summer at least one died from jumping off the bridge, just to prove that they could. But not this early in the year, and not on a weekday. Sometimes you are ready for the sirens and sometimes you are not.

"Hey girlie!" Courtney said when she saw April. "No runny today?"

"Nope," April said. One-word answers between the girl and her stepmother were not uncommon. When Marcus had first brought home the young, pretty woman, Joan had felt threatened, and worried that the role she'd played in the girl's life would be eclipsed by someone newer, hipper, more interesting. She was secretly delighted that April felt much the same about Courtney as she herself did. She'd tolerate her, and concealed her distain, but didn't really make much of an effort beyond that.

"Did you hear about that boy who drowned?" April asked Joan.

"I did. Isn't that sad?"

"Okay," April said and leaned conspiratorially close to her grandmother. "Here's the scoop. I *knew* him."

"You did?"

"Yeah, he went to my school. I didn't know him real good. He was kind of quiet, you know, but I knew him to see him and Carly sat beside him in band class. He played the *trumpet.*" April said trumpet as though that was somehow significant, but Joan couldn't see how.

"Oh. Was he any good?"

"I don't know, Granny. Geez. What a thing to ask!" April took out a worksheet from her folder that appeared to be some sort of math. Joan hoped the girl wouldn't ask her for any help.

"Sorry."

"I heard he was down at the river with two of his friends, one of them is older and has a car. So stupid. Like, what are you doing swimming in the middle of the night anyway?"

"Water can sure be dangerous," Joan said. A million stories popped into her mind of drownings and almost drownings. There was that Miller man who died in Decker's Creek when he jumped in to save his little boy. That boy drowned too, come to think of it. And her own second cousin lost her mind for a little while and had to go to the state hospital when the boy she was engaged to drowned in Ohio where he was working. She was about to tell April one of these stories when Courtney came back to the table and sat down.

"What's shaking, Chickie?" she asked April. "Have you ever seen this show? If you were going on it, what would you be?"

"I don't know," April said. "Maybe a goose."

"A goose? Like, all fat and white? Like Mother Goose."

"No," April said and smiled up at Joan. "Like the goose who laid the golden egg. Get it?"

Joan's heart swelled with love for the little girl. She laughed and slapped the table. "Now, that's an episode I might watch," she said. Courtney looked confused, even though the name of the bar was printed on the napkin her glass of iced tea was sweating into. That made Joan laugh harder.

"Hey, I like your eyes," Courtney said and leaned close to April, as if to inspect the makeup. "Did you use the one I gave you?"

"Yeah," April said, and smiled. "Lots of my friends said they liked my makeup today. Even one of the teachers." Joan's full heart squeezed a little and started to deflate. "Thanks!"

"Sure thing! I have some lipstick too that I don't use if you want it."

"Don't you think she's a little too young?" Joan spat, not able to control herself any longer.

"Nah," Courtney said. "All the girls are doing it now. It's just a little makeup."

"Yeah, Grandma. It's just a little makeup," April said. Joan saw her and Courtney share a knowing look—a look about her.

"Did you hear about that kid that got drowned, Courtney?" April was asking. "I *knew* him."

"No way!" Courtney said and leaned even closer to April.

"Yeah! He played the *trumpet* in the *band*."

"Whoa," Courtney said.

"I think those people want to order now, Courtney," Joan said, motioning toward the one table of people in the restaurant, people who seemed uninterested in their menus or in ordering any food.

"Oh," Courtney said, getting up reluctantly. "Okay."

"Granny," April said. "When are you going to start letting me work here for real?"

"Filling salt shakers and marrying the ketchup ain't good enough for you anymore?"

"I could use the money, and I know this place better'n just about anybody. I could do it." The thought of what her little granddaughter might need money for rattled Joan to the core. More makeup? Tight pants? Or worse things like maybe what that little boy was doing out with someone who could drive a car, things that ended him up dead in the river. The thought came to her to ask April if she knew anyone who drove a car, but she bit down on her tongue again.

"Well, we'll see in another year, okay? But there ain't much to do except in the nighttime, and you know you ain't working then."

"Oh, Granny," April said and rolled her eyes hard to the ceiling. She settled into her math work and Joan watched her for a minute, remembered the chubby-thighed little thing that used to toddle around The Egg, back when Joan's husband was still alive and tending bar. April's mama was still around then, too, and would let the baby roll pool balls across the floor as she wiped down tables. That was before she got more interested in other things, like the men and what they could do for her, what they could give her that Marcus couldn't or wouldn't. She and Marcus were too young to get married, but once you have a baby, you grow up. That's what Joan knew to be true, but it doesn't happen for everybody, and April didn't much seem to miss her mama. Joan worried that one day the woman would show back up—still skinny and strung out, or worse, pretty again with her life back together—and want to take April away.

When her second cousin's man died in Ohio, Joan went to the funeral. The whole family did. She was only sixteen then and looked a lot like April did now. When Cousin Mary saw Joan, she grabbed her by the hands and squeezed, hard. "It's so fast," Mary said. "You think you got a hold of it, that maybe you can make sense of the world, but it just spins and spins and spins, so fast. You think you got something, but what you got is a handful of shit. That's all life is. A big handful of shit." She wouldn't let go of Joan's hands; she squeezed and squeezed until tears were in both their eyes. Finally, Joan's father pried the woman's hands away. What Joan would always remember most wasn't her words, though, or the pain in her hands, but the look on Cousin Mary's face when she walked away. She'd just given up. She'd found the answer: that nothing really mattered.

"They're ghosts," she said as her own parents led her away. "And they don't care."

II.

The note was lying right on the little shelf inside her locker. Someone had pushed it through the holes in the door. It could have been there for days because Carly hardly ever went to her locker. There wasn't much time between classes and she could just carry most of her books.

She didn't know how long it had been there, but she found it on the morning they all heard about the boy's death. And when she opened the note—just a piece of lined notebook paper folded in half—and saw that it was from him, she ran to the girls' bathroom and threw up all over the floor of stall number two.

"Someone's in there hurling," a girl said as she opened the bathroom door, then quickly left. Carly knew the girl was probably going to get a teacher, and she didn't want to answer any questions, so she picked herself up, and darted out the door.

She didn't know the boy all that well, really. They sat next to each other in band. They shared a music stand. He played okay, just like she played okay. Just like most of them played okay. They were kids and none of them really had a passion for music, and that's why the band teacher yawned through most of his conducting. At the end of this year, the band would go to Kennywood and ride roller coasters while the chaperones sneaked cigarettes, and then it would be over. She'd go on to high school and never really think much about the trumpet or sheet music or quarter notes again.

"Dear Carly," the note had started. Once she got home, she locked herself in the upstairs bathroom and read it again and again. "Hi. How are you? I hope you are good. I am good." He wrote in pencil, and she noticed how he'd erased and rewritten his words a few times, probably to make them as neat as possible. He'd also carefully removed the little edges from where the paper was ripped from the spiral notebook, and that touched her heart. She hated those edges, the way they looked messy and would catch on everything. Most boys didn't even try to remove them and her teachers would always complain, but this boy was clearly different.

"Do you like that play that we are reading in English class? I do not know if I do or if I don't, but it did get me thinking some about how maybe we should not waste time and that we should just say what we mean. Do you think that way too? I think you do. I wanted to say to you that I like you very much. That your hair is pretty and that you smell good. You do not have to say anything back to me. I just wanted you to know because I thought maybe you didn't."

Carly's hair was wild and curly. No matter how she tried to tame it, it stuck up in unruly spirals, frizzy and loud. There were many shiny-haired girls at the school, the pretty ones who wore the right clothes and who danced like they knew what they were doing; Carly was not one of those girls. Those girls probably got love notes all the time, but Carly had never got as much as a nonrequired Valentine's Day card.

They'd been reading *Our Town* in seventh period. The teacher, Ms. Fultz, loved it and wanted the class to love it too. "It's simple, but it's so beautiful," she kept saying. The kids thought it was boring. They kept waiting for something big to happen and when it never did, they got surly and refused even to answer her questions about how the text made them *feel*. "But don't you see, guys?" she had said, and the pleading in her voice just made everything so much worse. "It's about life."

"Can't we read something scary, Ms. Fultz?" one boy asked. Ms. Fultz looked like she wanted to cry, and Carly felt bad for her, so the next day, when Ms. Fultz asked for volunteers to read aloud, Carly volunteered to be Emily. They were nearing the end of the play, the part where Emily has died but the Stage Manager takes her back to her birthday, for one final look at her family.

Carly read the part where Emily asks her mother to just really look at her.

"Ms. Fultz," Carly asked, pausing in her reading. Tyler James was popping gum and two or three kids had their heads down on their desks, either sleeping or pretending to. Ms. Fultz, though, had shiny eyes and was looking at Carly as though she really was that poor dead Emily.

"Yes?" Ms. Fultz said, blinking away her dreamy tears.

"Is Emily wanting her mom to see her ghost, like now that she's dead, or is she wanting her to see her, like to know who she really is? Or does Emily just want her to see her because then she'd feel alive again?"

It was a good question, Carly thought. It sounded smart, unlike when she usually tried to ask something and it came out jumbled and confused.

"Well," Ms. Fultz said, and then paused in a way that made Carly think that she didn't really know. "What do you think?"

Carly thought about being invisible. About how she never saw the boy who put that note in her locker. He saw her, and she didn't even know. And now he was dead, maybe a ghost like Emily, standing next to her desk shouting, beating his chest, begging just once for her to really look at him.

"I don't know," she said, and shrugged her shoulders. Brian Bee was tapping his pencil against his cheek, making a *plunk, plunk, plunk* sound. Christy yawned loudly.

She tried hard to think of him, to remember his hair and his eyes. If she'd ever noticed what he smelled like, or a particular way that he held his trumpet. But all she could get was a general picture of his face, like something that would be in the yearbook, and an image of his shoes, dirty and brown, ugly and cheap, next to hers as they tapped out the rhythm of their song.

"Would you like to keep reading, Carly?" Ms. Fultz asked.

"No," Carly said, feeling the bile rising in her throat again. "I think I'm done."

III.

If I had taken three steps, if I had longer legs, if my shoes weren't the cheap ones from the Walmart but the cool ones from the mall, if Billy had been closer, if it hadn't rained, if I hadn't gotten into Billy's brother's car, if my dad hadn't gone bowling, if my mom hadn't taken her sleeping pill early, if Billy hadn't put that note in Carly's locker, if my balance was better, if I was an athlete instead of a band geek, if I didn't play the trumpet, maybe I wouldn't have fell.

The falling was the worst part because it was so fast and so slow, but when I hit that water, there was a rock, I think, or something hard—maybe the bottom of the Earth itself, and my head hit it and I don't remember. My body is not me now. I do not feel tied to it. I am not wet or dripping. I am awake and I am asleep. I am everywhere and I am nowhere.

If I am a ghost, I will haunt the river. Maybe I will be in one of those "ghosts of West Virginia" books and people will tell my story. Or they'll tell a story about me because no one will really know what happened. Maybe some people will think that Billy pushed me in, or that I tried to push him in because I was angry about the note he slipped in Carly's locker. I wrote it, but I would never have put it in there. I just wanted to see what the words looked like on the paper. I just wanted to know how it would feel to write them. But then he saw that note and thought it would be so funny if he just shoved that right in her face. But she wasn't in school that afternoon because she'd gone to the orthodontist, so instead he put it in her locker. I wanted it back, but a locker is locked and there was no getting it. Then days went by and we sat next to each other in band, and she didn't say a word. She must have been so embarrassed, so disgusted or ashamed, that she couldn't even look at me. But it doesn't matter now. I'm not sad, or scared, or tired, or embarrassed. I am just.

When I fell, did I hear Billy scream? I think I did. He was right behind me because he is my friend and he would not let me go out on that bridge rail alone. I thought he was right behind me, but when I fell, I looked up and I didn't see him. Maybe I didn't see him, or maybe I was falling too fast and I didn't look in the right place. I never look in the right place. But I know he didn't push me because if he had, I would have seen him when I looked up. It doesn't matter now. And if what I felt was a hand that was pushing, and not a hand that was holding, that doesn't matter either.

Billy's brother had the camera, and he was filming us. "We'll put it on YouTube," Billy said. I didn't want to because I was afraid, and that me didn't understand like this me does that fear is not real. But Billy said that maybe Carly would see it, and I thought about how she sat by me every day and never mentioned that note, and I thought about how her lips looked when she pressed them tight to the mouthpiece of the trumpet. Sometimes, I'd watch her and then I'd press my lips to my mouthpiece, but I would imagine that cold to be her warm lips, and no notes would come out, and Mr. Shaffer would give me that look that said, "Just what I thought."

The embouchure is important to playing correctly. You have to put your lips just right, apply just the right amount of pressure, so that the right sound will come from the end of the horn. Mr. Shaffer tells us that if we press too hard, it will ruin our lips. He had a friend once, he says, who had played trombone for years. He was in a car accident and his lip busted and inside was black bloody goo. "Bad embouchure," Mr. Shaffer says.

When they find my body, if they do, I hope they will cut open my lips to see what is inside. Lips are as important as a heart and a brain and a lung. Maybe there will be some secret there, like the trombone player's secret. He always pressed too hard. I said too much, or not enough, or my shoes were wrong, or I misstepped. It was an accident. It was on purpose. It has to be one or the other.

I wrote the note, but Billy tore off the edges of the paper before putting it in Carly's locker.

How long will I be here and not here? Long enough to haunt the boys who come to walk the bridge rail, or the girl with coiled hair who throws flowers into the water? Billy and Carly, holding hands? I am slipping in and out. They do not see me. I am in between.

Get Up, June

———

My father was a man of addictions. When I was little, it was booze. He nearly drank himself to death, my mom says, but I don't remember much of that. Mostly what I remember was him wrecking cars. He always said that he swerved to miss a deer. Somehow, he never once got hurt.

When I was in the sixth grade, he started with the drug tests. The pharmaceutical company would pay him a couple hundred dollars to take a new drug for a couple months. The side effects were often horrible—intense vomiting, skin rashes, hallucinations. Once, he came into my bedroom in the middle of the night, sweat running down his skinny face, his eyes wild. He was shouting at me that there were people in the house, people who had come to get us. I was so scared that I peed the bed. When I didn't move fast enough, he grabbed me by the ankle and started pulling me.

"Get up, June. Get up!" He was screaming, and I was wrapped up in my blankets, grabbing on to anything I could to keep him from getting me.

Finally, my mom came, not rushing in like you might think, but just normal, looking tired and annoyed. "Come on, Michael," she said, touching his arm. "There ain't nobody in the house. Now, come on."

At first, he was doing it for the money, but then it was something else. It was the idea of seeing what would happen, I think, or of hoping something would happen that would change things.

Finally, he ended up in the hospital from a bad reaction, his face, hands, and feet swollen, purple, the skin nearly busting. That was the last time. The pharmaceutical company said he couldn't do it anymore because maybe his body chemistry had been compromised and he'd no longer be a good test subject.

Then, when I was a sophomore in high school, my father found Jesus. Or Jesus found him—that's what he'd say. A new church was built just outside of town—a massive, ugly structure, gray with industrial siding. The best part was the huge blue letters spelling JESUS that covered the front of the building, the side facing the road. "Good lord," my mom said, the first time she saw. "Now all they need are some neon lights."

They didn't get neon, but they did outline each of the letters with twinkle lights. Many, many strands of twinkle lights.

The sermons were usually about sin, sometimes about forgiveness. There were parables and the moral of the story. I was usually bored, picking at my fingernails or looking through the ratty little Bible for curse words. My father, though, would intensely watch the preacher. He'd rock back and forth in the pew. Sometimes, he'd whisper "amen" or "thank you, Jesus" softly so only my mom and I could hear. Toward the end of our time at the Jesus church, he started shouting, feeling moved by the spirit. Once, he left the pew and ran up and down the aisles. I was scared, thought he was having an attack of some sort—maybe a leftover side effect from all those pharmaceuticals— but he was feeling the Lord, touched by the hand of God.

It was much later that I learned that my father had been giving most of his paycheck to the Jesus church. He was working at my uncle's body shop then, doing oil changes and tune-ups. His paycheck hadn't been much, but over 60 percent went to the alms. He'd also been "spoken to" by the pastor and some of the head people at the Jesus church about his outbursts. Now, he wanted a place he could burst out any time he wanted to, any time the spirit moved him.

He got himself ordained.

I think for a while that he really believed it. And his belief was infectious. My whole life had taught me to be wary of him and his passions, but other people came to him. He would hold a little service in the backyard if the weather was nice, and in the garage of his brother's body shop when it wasn't. People started calling him to preach at weddings and funerals. He would tell stories about Samson and Delilah, and Daniel, and David. My mom and I went with him at first, but then it was just me. This is when I first realized that people don't really listen to the words preachers say, they don't think too hard about it. I knew he got things wrong—all the time—but no one else seemed to know it. Samson and Delilah really was a love story. My dad never recognized the sacrifice.

His church meetings got stranger and stranger. He asked for those who felt they needed special prayer to come forward, and he'd lay his hands on their head. He'd touch his forehead to their forehead, and they'd cry together. Sometimes people talked in tongues, babbling and reaching up to the sky. They'd take off running, too, like he did that last time in the Jesus church. It was scary, but fascinating, and I couldn't stop going.

"June, don't you feel anything at the service?" he'd asked as we drove home from the body shop in his rusty pickup.

"What do you mean?" I asked.

"Doesn't the Lord ever move you? Don't you ever get the spirit?"

"I don't know," I said. "What does it feel like?"

He thought about it for a minute, then said, "Well, it's different every time. Sometimes it comes into my legs, a tingling, and a burning, and I just have to move. Sometimes it comes in my arms and I have to raise them to God. Sometimes it comes in my chest and it squeezes and squeezes until I have to let it out through my tears."

"Are you sure you're not having a heart attack?" I asked. My smart mouth was regularly getting me into trouble by that time.

"I worry about you, June," he said. "I worry that you will never find God, and that you will someday be a wanton woman."

"Wouldn't God still love me?"

"He might," my father mumbled, "but I don't know if I could."

My mother said if he started collecting rattlesnakes and copperheads, she was leaving him.

At first, the congregation grew quickly, but eventually it was just the same thirty or so people each week. I don't know where those people thought the crumpled dollars they put in the collection plate were going, but they went right into my father's pocket. They bought our groceries and paid our telephone bill. It didn't seem right, but I needed those things, too, so never once said anything.

When my dad preached, his face would get red. He'd scream and hop around on one foot (when the spirit was in his legs). He'd spit his words out so hard that actual spit would fly onto the people sitting in the first row of folding chairs. At home, he'd practice in the back bedroom, and I'd sneak outside and around the back of the house so that I could watch him. The first time, though, he'd just say the sermon like any normal person, but then he'd work himself up. He'd start breathing heavy and do the little dance. It was all a performance, and if he had to practice getting moved by the spirit, I couldn't believe that it was real.

I couldn't reconcile how I felt at the church meetings with what I knew about my father to be true. I didn't get moved by the Lord to run through the aisles or speak in a strange tongue, but I was fascinated, and could never look away. These people had found my father because they were lost. I saw that in myself too. When he touched their faces, just that little bit of humanity touched them so deep that tears squeezed out of their eyes. I wanted to feel that too. It couldn't be all bad, even if it wasn't true.

One night, my dad brought out dish pans and filled them with water. He asked that we wash each other's feet, just like Jesus washed the feet of his disciples. "When Simon Peter asked Jesus why he was washing his feet, the Lord said, 'Unless I wash you, you have no part with me,'" he said as he poured water from old milk jugs into the pans. "I'll start. Jesus said, 'You call me "Teacher" and "Lord," and rightly so, for that is what I am. Now that I, your Lord and Teacher, have washed your feet, you also should wash one another's feet. I have set you an example that you should do as I have done for you. Very truly I tell you, no servant is greater than his master, nor is a messenger greater than the one who sent him.'"

The men rolled up their pants' legs and went first. My father took his hands and cupped water, then let it dribble over each man's foot. He'd put rags in the pans, but didn't use them himself. The women seemed more hesitant, but finally got in line behind the men and let my father run his rough hands over each of their feet. Corrine Reese was standing in front of me. She was only a few years older than me, had left high school the year before because she was pregnant. I knew she had a little baby girl and a husband who didn't come to our church. When my father touched her foot, she shivered. She had long, straight hair all the way down to her butt, and I watched it ripple. I remembered the story of the woman washing Jesus's feet with her tears, then drying them with her long, long hair.

"June, you're next," he said. I didn't want to, but everyone was watching me, and it was clear they wouldn't get on with washing one another's feet until I'd had my turn.

I stood on one leg, and offered my right foot to my father, who took it in one hand and dribbled the cold water over it with the other. As he circled his hand around my ankle, I felt pulled again, like the night when he tried to drag me from my bed, and a sob rose.

He rubbed the sole of my foot, pressing his thumb into my arch, then leaned his head down and gently kissed the top. "I love you, June," he said very quietly as he released one foot and waited for me to offer him the other. As he took it, he whispered, "I love you, my child, as God loved his only son."

When Jesus washed the feet of his disciples, he told them that he could not make them all clean.

We pulled the metal chairs around the pans, four or five that my father had set out and filled, then took turns with one another. No one said we had to, but the men went with the men and the women with the women. It was so odd, seeing these men who usually look so grown, so strong and tough, doing something tender for each other.

I sat in the chair and Corrine Reese kneeled in front of me. No one was talking to one another, but the hushed sounds of whispered prayers filled the garage like air. I remembered seeing Corrine at school, before she got pregnant and left. She was pretty, and in my memory, light bounced around her shoulders and reflected off her shield of hair. My hair was mousy brown and stringy, always falling into my eyes, greasy where I would push at it and tuck it behind my ears. I couldn't offer her my foot, even though she sat there, waiting. Finally, she had to take my ankle in her hands and lift my foot from the floor.

The water was shockingly cold as she ran the rag over my toes, up toward my ankle. I could feel her fingers as she held me. My chest was tight and suddenly I wanted nothing more than to feel Corrine's hair on my skin, to use it to dry the tears. Jesus was just a man, and as godly as he might have been, he must have craved human touch, the sweet pleasure in having someone else touch you in a kind way. My father never would have believed this.

When we switched places, Corrine offered me her foot with a smile. I wasn't quite sure what to do, and when I lifted the rag, I washed her foot as though I was washing my own in the shower, scrubbing and pushing the rag between her toes. She giggled a little when I dragged the rag across the bottom. "God bless you, Corrine," I mumbled and pushed her foot away. I knew that I had not done the same gentle service for her that she had done for me.

———————

I had a boyfriend for a while that year. His name was Brian and he lived a little ways up the windy dirt road from us. His hair was buzzed short and I didn't like how I could see his scalp right through it. There was something too vulnerable about that, and it made me uncomfortable.

Brian was scared of my dad. He'd hold my hand, but only when no one else could see. He kissed me once on the cheek, and when I turned my head to kiss his mouth, he stepped back and said, "I dunno, June. Maybe we better not. Your daddy'd get mad."

"Who gives a shit about my daddy?" I asked.

"He's crazy," Brian said, his green eyes wide. "Everybody says so."

When he started having people to the house for private Bible lessons, Mom started going to bingo. She wanted me to come along, but I said I didn't want to. Instead I'd walk down the hill and sit with my grandma who'd been feeling sick most of the spring. The skin on her hands was getting so papery thin that I could see all the veins right through.

One evening, when I walked back up from Grandma's, I saw Corrine's husband's old truck out in front of the house. It was one of those very high, off-the-ground ones, and I tried to picture Corrine trying to pull herself up into it.

I went around the side of the house to the back window where I'd watch Daddy practice his sermons. I just wanted to see, to watch how he talked to Corrine. What I saw was Corrine lying on the bed, a wet rag over her face. She was crying, I could tell because her body rippled and shook. Daddy was standing over her. He must have been praying, but softly because I couldn't hear.

Daddy kneeled down next to the bed and put his hand on Corrine's leg. She was wearing a skirt that fell just to her knees, and

Daddy let his hand push up, over her knee, and slip under the hem. Corrine caught his wrist, but he said something to her, and he had a look on his face that I recognized—a look that said that he wasn't to be stopped, that you shouldn't even try. He looked up to the ceiling again, and his mouth made a prayer. Even though I couldn't hear him, I knew this is what he did. Corrine released his wrist and let her arm drape over her eyes. Daddy's hand went higher and higher. The sinner in me wanted to watch, but for Corrine, I didn't. I ran up the hill to find Brian, to tell him to stop being scared of my father. Daddy wasn't crazy, and he wasn't godly. He was just like the rest of us, weak and pathetic. I went to tell Brian that I wanted to be a wanton woman, a trashy whore. Maybe I already was.

I'd like to say that this was the last straw—that I told Mom and we left my father to his addictions, but I'd be lying. For months I kept the secret. I sneaked out my window and met Brian in the woods. I'd pull myself on top of him and tell him not to think about God but the devil as I bit down on his lip. If he wasn't scared before, he sure was now, but his fear for my daddy wasn't as strong as I was.

I wasn't a stupid girl. I knew how babies were made. I just didn't care.

Don't worry. This isn't that story.

One day a congregation member called our house. We were sitting at the dinner table, just starting to eat the sad meatloaf my mother had thrown together without much effort. The ketchup on top looked like blood and I was thinking that maybe I'd just have mashed potatoes. She answered the phone, then silently handed it to my daddy with an annoyed sigh.

There'd been an accident. The niece of Bobby Gibson had hit a tree and was thrown from the car onto some rocks along the side of Route 7. Would Daddy come to the hospital and pray with her family?

"Come along, June," he said. I told him that I didn't want to, but he gave me the look, and I knew there wasn't an option.

The girl was about my age, probably a couple years older. She lived in the next county, so I didn't recognize her. She was lying in the bed, tubes down her throat and in her arms. She was blonde, but otherwise could have been me lying there, looking like a little kid in a grown-up's bed.

There was a priest in the room when we first got there, and Daddy and I stood outside, waiting for him to get done. "Bobby said she was Catholic on her mama's side," he said, "but her daddy don't hold with that."

The priest read to the girl from his little Bible. He drew from a vial of oil and marked the girl's forehead and wrists. The priest's voice was soft, and he asked the family to join him in saying the Lord's Prayer. I joined them too, but only moved my lips so my father wouldn't hear.

When the priest left, Daddy and I entered, and he went right to the girl and took her hand. He started praying, saying, "Lord, Lord, please hear me. Please hear me, Lord, and heal this girl. This girl is young, Lord, she is strong, but her body is weak. Jesus, Jesus, Jesus." I stood behind him, watching the girl's parents. Grief poured out of them; it filled up the room.

There was a smell, like dried shit, and I saw the bag of brown liquid near the floor, connected to a hose that went up under the sheets. I was sick to my stomach, not because of the smell, but because I was smelling it. I was ashamed for the girl, embarrassed for her that she had strangers smelling her smell and seeing that soft, thin-skinned part of her collarbone that only someone who loved her should get to see. We should not have been there. I should not have been there.

My daddy was touching the girl, first one wrist and then the other; then he laid the heels of both hands on her forehead. I finally realized that he was rubbing off the priest's oil, trying to take away the Catholic anointing.

"Stop it," I hissed, trying to keep the girl's parents from hearing. All I could think about was his hands, running up under Corrine Reese's skirt, and now wiping away something meant to be good.

"Good Lord, Jesus, Jesus, Jesus. Please hear me tonight. I am your humble servant, Lord, here with my good little daughter. Help this family through this troubled time."

"Stop it," I said again, a little louder, and I saw the mother's eyes flick to me.

"Oh!" My father jumped back and grabbed his chest. "I feel it," he said. "I feel the Lord moving in me. Thank you, Jesus."

He was breathing heavy, and bent over. He was holding on to me, as if to keep from falling.

"Are you okay?" The girl's father asked.

"She spoke to me," my father said, quietly first, then louder. "She spoke to me and said, 'Let me go, Mommy. Let me go, Daddy. The Lord is calling me home.'" The woman wailed then, a wail like I had never heard, and collapsed into the man's arms. They both fell down together onto the hard tile floor, a crying pile of tangled arms and legs.

"Come now, June. Let's leave the family to their own." Daddy turned to leave the room, but I couldn't make my feet move. The sobbing man and woman, this poor girl that could be me, they'd trapped me in the room and in their web of grief. I couldn't breathe. My feet wouldn't carry me.

"I did say come along, June," Daddy said, and grabbed my arm. He pulled me from the room and toward the elevator.

"I never want to come with you again," I mumbled as we waited on the elevator. "That was wrong."

"What was so wrong? We helped those people." The elevator arrived, and the doors creaked open. My father was humming as he stepped on. I could not imagine following him and being trapped with him in that small space. "Get on, girl," he said.

"You didn't help them," I said. "That girl didn't talk to you."

"Who is to say she didn't?" He had his arm in the elevator door, holding it open, but I could tell that he was losing patience with me.

"Me. I say she didn't. I know she didn't."

"Look," he said. "That girl ain't ever gonna wake up. The quicker her folks realize that, the better. I helped them realize it. What difference does it make how?"

"You lied."

"We all lie. Now get on the goddamn elevator."

What I wanted to say is this: "I don't want to be like you."

This is what I said: "I'm taking the stairs."

That night, I told my mother about Corrine Reese and Daddy in the back bedroom. She didn't cry like I thought most women would, and said she was pretty sure she already knew, and that it likely wasn't only that "poor, simple girl" Corrine. Then I told her about Daddy and the girl at the hospital. I told her about Brian, too, because I couldn't stop talking. That was when she cried, and pulled me close to her.

"Please," I said. "Please." I didn't know what I was asking for, but she did, finally.

She told my daddy she was done. "Go live with one of your whores," she said, but none of them would have him because they all had husbands. Instead, he ended up just down the hill, sleeping on my grandma's couch as she quietly died in the other room.

"June," my mother said to me one day, not long after she'd kicked my father out. "I hope you will not forget the good parts of your daddy. His kindness. His determination. I hope you will take those good parts of him and the good parts of me, and try to push out the bad parts. Will you do that?"

"I'll try," I said, and thought about Daddy, just a little ways away down the hill. I will try, but at the heart of me, I know he's always within reach.

At the Lake

———

When I was a kid, we didn't take long car rides for the heck of it, or eat fast food. I wore my brother's hand-me-down clothes, and he sometimes wore my dad's. My mom got her hair done in town at the Sit 'n Set instead of one of the nicer places at the mall or in the JC Penney's. The one time of the whole year that we did something just for our family—and just for fun—was the week in the summer that we spent at the lake. Every Fourth of July, we rented the same little cabin and would drive the two hours to Teeters Lodge. We'd spend the week feeling like rich folks, lounging around, swimming, doing just about everything we could outside, and letting the sun heat us up from the outside in. Sometimes I felt like I soaked that sun in, stored it up so that it could carry me through all those months ahead. We went every year, until the year that my brother Ben was sixteen and I was thirteen. This was the year my brother's girlfriend came to the lake with us, and never went home.

I don't have to spend time waxing poetic on how much I looked up to my brother. You all know that story already and can fill in the blanks however you want. Here are a few things to get you going: Ben was tall and narrow, tanned in the summer as brown as a berry.

His hair was lighter than mine and cut close to his head. Mine was always flopping around and in my eyes. He was smart and funny, and never got annoyed with my hanging around. He liked history and was going to join one of those groups that did Civil War reenactments, and he would be on the Confederate side because they never had enough. Pictures: me riding on handlebars; me and him sitting on the pier, feet dangling in the green water, fishing for bluegill or trout, but catching only a snapping turtle; Ben looking into a sparkler on the Fourth of July, his face too close to the hot light, but not moving back; me, standing on the porch and looking after Ben and Carrie as they walked away, their fingers just barely touching.

Carrie was Ben's first girlfriend, I think. At least the first out-of-school one who would come to our house for dinner some nights and who he'd walk home. I knew they had kissed one night that spring in our backyard because I saw them out the window of the bedroom my brother and I shared. When he came upstairs, I made smooching noises and he threw a pillow at my head.

I thought Carrie was pretty, with her straight blond hair that hung all the way to her butt, and her long legs. She was little, too, hardly up to my brother's shoulder. That made me feel like she was someplace in between Ben and me, and that made me like her more. She was also not like the other girls. She wore black a lot, and usually long sleeves even when it was warm. Sometimes Ben would tell my mom about how Carrie got in fights with her parents. Ben and Carrie might have told my parents this as a scheme to soften them. Whether that was the goal or not, it must have worked, because my mom and dad agreed to let Carrie come with us to the lake.

I think we were all surprised, and I was immediately angry. I'd asked just the summer before for Caleb, my then best friend, to come with us and had been given a swift no. "This is family time," my dad had said, and that was the end of the discussion.

"What about family time?" I asked when Mom announced at dinner one night that she and Dad had decided Carrie could come.

"Well, Carrie is like family," she said, and I rolled my eyes. I liked Carrie well enough, but I liked her in Rawlings, where she spent maybe two hours in my life, and then went home. I didn't like her at the lake, and I didn't like what her being at the lake was going to mean.

"Look, Joshy," Mom said later that night when we were alone. "Ben is getting older, and things are going to change. He'll always be your brother, and he'll always love you, but you'll have to let go a little. Understand?"

"You know they'll probably have sex at the lake," I said. I hadn't meant to say it, but it just came out. That spring, I'd sat red faced and twitchy in Mr. Bottoms's class as he gave all the boys "the talk." Ever since then, I'd been wanting to ask Ben if he and Carrie were doing it, or when they were going to, because Mr. Bottoms said that teenagers were all like sneaky monkeys, always trying to find some hideout to "do it" in.

"Josh!" My mother, understandably, was horrified, and slapped me hard across the leg. It didn't hurt, but I buried my face in my pillow anyway.

"Someday, you'll understand why your dad and I have made this decision," she said after taking a few calming breaths. "And you'll hope that we'll make the same decision for you."

My parents were happy that Ben had a girlfriend. Too happy, really, and now I realize that Ben with a girl—especially a pretty girl like Carrie—had eased some fear they'd had about him. He was gangly and bookish, soft-spoken and shy. He was the kind of boy about whom my grandfather would say, "If he ain't queer, he's missing a good shot at it." When Ben brought home a girl, they could breathe a little easier and that question, it seemed, was answered.

So, perhaps my parents were too eager to please and weren't thinking clearly when they agreed to bring Carrie to the lake. It's true, they barely knew her, and had only talked to her mother on the phone for ten minutes. But when Carrie showed up at our house at 5:30 the morning that we were leaving for the lake, wearing a funny fisherman's hat and rolling a battered brown suitcase up our sidewalk, even I smiled, and maybe that was the moment that I fell in love with her too.

Carrie sat in the middle of the backseat, on the hump between me and Ben. She was wearing narrow jean shorts that came to her knees, and the skin on her legs was so shockingly white that I had to keep staring at it. Ben and Carrie were holding hands, and Carrie was talking fast, chattering about never getting to go anywhere with her family, and how excited she was to swim and see the fireworks over the water. I was brooding, feeling put out about not having enough room and being crowded against the window. Then, Carrie grabbed my hand and interlaced her fingers with mine. I started to yank my hand away, but her hand was warm and soft. She pulled the ball of our hands over into her lap, where it met the hand ball that she and Ben had made. I saw Ben glance over at me, but I couldn't read his expression. It wasn't angry, exactly, but it wasn't pleased, either. I decided to leave my hand right there with hers, and we rode like that all the way to the lake.

There was no lodge at Teeters Lodge, only six small cabins on 150 acres mostly circling the lake. Each cabin had enough land around it that you didn't have to see your neighbors if you didn't want to, and we never wanted to. The cabins were cheap enough because they were shoddy. Of course, now people would just call them rustic and charge even more for the experience of no air conditioning and the cracks in the walls. There were communal showers and bathrooms down close to the access road, but none in the cabins. There was, thankfully, running water and electricity to operate a little refrigerator that rattled all night long. There were two tiny bedrooms and a "family room," sparsely decorated with an old couch and two chairs—furniture that remained the same all the years we visited, except for looking a little sadder each year, and finally, the summer Carrie came with us, one of the legs fell off the brown chair. We sat in it anyway, lopsided, with one corner resting on the dusty wood floor. Ben and then Carrie on his lap, and then me, pulled down by her as I walked past. A giggling pile until Ben pushed us both off, hard, onto the floor. Carrie still laughed, but the look on Ben's face wasn't funny to me.

Maybe because she was always wearing long sleeves, the first time I saw Carrie in her bathing suit was shocking. Her arms were skinny, and every bit of her so white that she nearly glowed. She wore a sweatshirt down to the pier and only pulled it off as she got ready to jump into the water. Ben and I were already in the lake. It was our ritual to throw our bags in the cabin and dash to the pier, shedding clothes as we went. Years of experience had taught us to wear our swim shorts on the car ride to the lake so no time was wasted. Carrie, though, vacation newbie that she was, had to go into the tiny back bedroom that the three of us would share, and change.

Ben and I were hollering and splashing, trying to dunk each other in the cold lake water, until we saw Carrie tentatively at the end of the pier, her toes just barely over the edge. Her bathing suit was blue and she was so small that it sagged a little in the important places.

"Quit staring," Ben said and smacked the back of my head. I started to say that he was staring too, but didn't want another smack, and I guessed that it was okay for him since Carrie was his girlfriend.

"Is it cold?" Carrie shouted. She already looked freezing, her arms crossed around her chest and her skin so pale that she might have just been thawed out of a glacier.

"Some," Ben called back to her. "But it feels good. Hey Carrie, can you swim?"

"Not real good. I think I'll just dip my toe," she said and lowered herself down onto the pier. She let first one and then the other long leg over the edge. I watched as she dipped a toe, shivered, pulled it out, and then let her whole foot drop down into the water.

Ben started swimming back toward the shore, so I followed.

"Come on in," he said when he got closer to Carrie. He bobbed in the water by her submerged foot. Then, he touched the foot and ran his hand up her calf. I stayed back, feeling once again on the outside. I smacked the water. This is what I knew would happen. Ben and Carrie together, and me dogpaddling around the edges.

"No, not right now," Carrie said, and pretended like she was kicking Ben's hand away. He tugged her foot and she giggled. "Stop it," she said, and he tugged again, harder. I let myself float closer and saw the intense look on Ben's face. Carrie hadn't realized it yet, but Ben wasn't going to let her go. I knew that as sure as I knew when we wrestled around on the living-room floor that he wasn't going to let me up until he was good and ready. Even if I said *uncle*. Even if I cried.

Ben latched his hand around Carrie's other ankle and tugged again, pulling her forward on the pier.

"Ow!" Carrie said, not giggling anymore. "Come on, Ben. Stop it."

"Hey, Ben," I said. "Let's race. First one to the big rock wins."

"Not now, Josh," he said, not looking at me. He pulled Carrie's ankle again, hard enough to move her closer to the edge. "Carrie has to get wet. Think of it as an initiation, Carrie. You ain't one of us until you get in Coffin Lake."

"Coffin Lake?" Carrie said. She was smiling, but I could tell that it was a fake one. Her hands were scurrying around on the dock, trying to find a place to hold on. The lake was really called Coughlin Lake, but Ben had misheard when we were real little, and it had been Coffin Lake to us ever since. We used to tease each other: "Ew, don't swallow the Coffin water! You're going to be a zombie if you swallow the Coffin water."

Ben tugged her again, so hard that her butt bounced a little on the boards.

"Come on, Ben," Carrie said. "You're hurting me. Let go."

"I'm hurting you?" he asked, and floated closer. He let go of her ankle, and I was relieved. He moved closer still until her legs were on either side of his head, and he kissed the inside of her knee. Carrie laughed, also clearly relieved, and leaned forward as if to kiss him back. Just then, Ben thrust himself out of the water enough to grab her legs and push her off the pier. She was too surprised to scream, I think, her arms flailing and scraping her skin along the rough pier boards. Ben was laughing. I was too stunned to move.

Carrie went in face first, her cheek smacking the water. She came up quickly, but was splashing around, panicking and trying to keep her head above water.

"The water's not so deep there, Carrie," Ben said. "Just put your feet down and stand up." He was still holding on to one of the pier posts, bobbing up and down. No matter how old I get, how many years pass from that summer, I will never forget how his head bobbed above the water, like some floating thing not attached to a body beneath the lapping surface of Coffin Lake.

Carrie had landed close to me, so I paddled over to her. We were close to the same size, so I was able to grab hold of her. I didn't know what I was going to do exactly. I didn't know how to rescue anyone from drowning. I was just trying to calm her down. Ben forgot that Carrie was shorter than him. He might have been able to touch the bottom of the lake there, but I couldn't, and neither could she. Carrie wrapped her arms around my neck, so tightly that she was choking me. I quickly realized that in her panic, she was pushing me under.

"Carrie!" I said, sputtering on a mouthful of Coffin water. "You gotta stop that!" I had one arm around her waist and I made a move with my other arm to get us closer to shore, something like trying to swim, but it didn't really amount to anything. Instead of rescuing Carrie, I'd just created a bigger splashing mass of arms and legs.

I hadn't seen him come over to us, but Ben was there, and quickly untangled me from Carrie with a shove to my chest. Then Carrie's arms were around his neck and he was making his way in, walking as if it were so easy. He carried her up onto the little sandy shore. I thought for a moment that he was going to drop her into the grass, but he didn't. He laid her down carefully, and sat down next to her, stroking her arm and pushing her wet hair back from her face as she coughed. He'd wanted all along to save her, and I almost ruined it by doing it myself. One evil look from my brother as I collapsed, panting and exhausted, in the grass next to them told me that.

"I'm sorry, baby," Ben said to her. He kissed her shoulder and tried to hug her. She didn't push him away, but I could tell that her body was stiff and ungiving. Over his shoulder, she locked eyes with me, and it was fleeting, but I saw fear. Real fear. Then, I mistook it for shock from her near drowning, but now I realize that the fear was not of Coffin Lake, but of my brother. She was just learning to be afraid.

Carrie recovered quickly from her scare, and by that night was sitting around the campfire, licking chocolate from the s'mores from her fingers and asking me if I knew the words to "Kum Ba Yah."

"I know it's silly," she said, "but that's always what the perfect families do in the movies. Sit around the campfire and sing 'Kum Ba Ya.'"

I didn't know the words but wished so badly that I did that I almost made some up just to please her. Even though she'd been afraid in the water, and I had been too, I couldn't quit thinking about how it felt to have her arms, wet and cold, around my neck; her bare legs touching my bare legs; my arm around her waist. Just the memory of how her thin swimsuit moved under my hand made a thick lump rise in my throat.

Any time Ben caught me staring at Carrie, he'd shoot me a dirty look, or sock me hard in the shoulder.

We had some good days at the lake. Sometimes Ben and Carrie would disappear into the woods and come back looking happy and drunk, hair full of grass, dirt stains on the back of their shorts. I was a dumb kid, but even I had some vague idea of what they'd been doing. I still don't understand why my parents pretended not to notice, or why Carrie's parents had agreed to let her come. I didn't think much about it then. As a kid, you think you know everything, and that everything you want is also what's right, and that adults just don't get it. It's the adults' job, though, to protect kids from themselves. I don't think mine did their jobs, and neither did Carrie's.

As much as it annoyed Ben, Carrie tried to include me as much as she could. Sometimes she'd ask me to go on walks with them, then Ben would sulk and say he was going swimming instead. He was in the water a lot that summer, swimming long laps to the big rock and back. It never looked like he was having much fun; it was more like he was working.

When Carrie and I walked alone, we'd go farther than she and Ben, who I think usually just found a spot far enough away from the cabin so that they wouldn't be seen. I'd take her to the overlook where you could see down into the gulley. The trees were so green and thick. They looked like a blanket, soft and lush. Once Ben and I had seen an eagle—or at least we thought it was an eagle. I wanted to show that to Carrie so badly that my eyes were inventing fake eagles in every bird I saw.

"I love it here," she said. She was sitting on a rock, so close to the edge of the cliff that I was nervous. While she was afraid of the water, I had quickly realized that there wasn't much else that scared her, including the height of the gulley. "I wish I never had to leave."

"Maybe your family can come up here sometime," I said. I wanted to sit next to her, but my cautiousness kept me far away from the edge. "My family doesn't really go anywhere," she said.

"Why not?" I asked. Carrie shrugged a shoulder and stared out over the gap. There was so much in that shrug. Carrie, poised on the rock, so tiny and so big at the same time. That is a picture I pull from my memory over all the others. And there are others. There's her on the pier, my brother pulling her ankle; her eyes after he rescued her; Carrie with a wet rag in the bedroom, wiping at the painful scrapes on the backs of her legs. I suppose I didn't do a very good job of protecting her either, but I was just a kid. Isn't that the embarrassing, shameful thing we always say? I was just a kid.

"Josh, come help me up," Carrie said, and motioned me closer to the edge. She held out her hand. I inched my way toward her and put my hand in hers. I was afraid that she would pull me, trying to get me closer to the edge. That's what Ben would have done. But Carrie just smiled and pulled herself up. When she got to her feet, she didn't let go of my hand, and she held it all the way back to the cabin. We swung our arms and talked about things like what teachers she hoped she got the next year and how she liked the fast roller coasters at Kennywood, but not the tall ones. I wanted to ride a roller coaster with Carrie. I wanted to see her hair flying and hear her screaming with pure joy. I hated roller coasters, but I would ride one with Carrie.

When we got back to the cabin, still holding hands and swinging arms, Ben was on the porch, looking annoyed and sunburned. Carrie's face broke into a big smile when she saw him, but froze when she saw the expression on his face.

"Where have you been?" he said, stomping toward us.

"I took her to the overlook," I said.

"Shut up," he said to me, but glared at Carrie. He grabbed her wrist and yanked her hand free from mine.

"Ben! Jesus, calm down," I said. Normally I would not talk back to my brother, but I was emboldened by Carrie, by the memory of touching her skin all the way from the overlook.

Ben turned on me then. "I said to shut up, Joshy. No one asked you." He pushed me hard in the middle of my chest, so hard that I fell back and landed on my butt in the grass. I wasn't hurt, but embarrassed to be revealed as an obvious child, manhandled by my skinny-armed older brother.

"I want to talk to you," Ben said to Carrie and dragged her back toward the cabin. "I brought you up here to be with me," I heard him say. "Not to make out with my little brother."

"Don't be stupid," she said. "He's just a kid. We were just having fun." That was the last thing I heard them say before they disappeared around the side of the cabin, headed toward the lake. It was enough, though, enough to make me feel like something ripped inside my stomach, a pain that shot though my chest and brought tears to my eyes.

That night Carrie was quiet and at the bonfire sat with her arms wrapped around her knees, staring into the flames. I was quiet, too, but no one seemed to notice. The absence of Carrie's chatter, her questions and giggles, was more obvious. Even my father, who had mostly ignored Carrie and Ben since we'd arrived, tried talking to her.

"What are your folks doing this holiday weekend, Carrie?" he asked.

"Oh, I don't know," she said. "Probably nothing. They might take my little sister down to the park to see the fireworks. We do that sometimes." My ears perked up. This was the first mention I'd heard of a little sister. I wondered how old she was. She must have been younger than me because there was no one with Carrie's last name in my grade.

"Oh, that sounds nice," my mother said. "I miss that. Here we just put off our own little fireworks, you know, which is nice but it's not the same."

"Remember that year when that neighbor kid nearly blew his hand off?" Ben said. He, unlike Carrie, was full of conversation. It was like they had switched personalities. He was sitting close to her, had part of him touching her at all times. I noticed that they didn't hold hands, though. It was more Ben touching Carrie than Carrie touching back. "Remember that they had to get that ambulance up here and how long it took? I bet that kid lost his whole hand, don't you think?"

"Christ, Ben," Dad said. "That was terrible. Why bring that up?"

"I don't know," Ben said, tossing a rock into the fire. The sparks flew up and danced brightly into the night sky. "Because it was some excitement."

"That's a terrible thing to say, Ben," my mother said. "That poor boy. I haven't seen that family back since."

I didn't know it then, but we wouldn't be back either. After that summer, Teeters Lodge and Coffin Lake would be gone for us, and we would be the family others told stories about as they sat around the campfire. Another family would move into our summer cabin, laugh as they sat in the chair without a leg. Another set of brothers would race to the big rock, dare each other to jump off.

That year, the Fourth was on a Saturday, and we'd leave the next day, headed back to our normal life of me and Ben in a too-small room, Carrie at home with her parents and little sister. That morning was beautiful, sunny and warm but not too hot. I got up early because I wanted to swim in the lake by myself while Ben snored. I noticed that Carrie was gone too. She'd been sleeping in the top bunk, and Ben slept on the bottom. I, of course, had a sleeping bag on the floor, but I didn't mind because from there I could see Carrie. She slept like a broken doll, twisted and tangled, her head thrown over the side, hair dangling.

That morning I came upon Carrie sitting in the grass, looking at the bottom of her bare foot. The bugs had been eating Carrie alive— mosquitos and gnats and wasps. I'd often see her digging at an ankle or an elbow. Sometimes Ben would sit behind her and scratch the bumps on her back. Once, I even caught her with a stick, pushing at some hard-to-reach itch. That morning, it was a bumblebee. It had been lying in the grass, and she'd stepped on it.

"I know I should have been wearing shoes," she said when she saw me. Fat tears ran down her cheek, and tears sprang to my eyes too, in sympathy. I knew just how bad that hurt because I'd done it myself, that white hot pain and then the itch that you can't quite find to scratch.

"Come on back to the house and we'll put something on it," I said, trying to sound like a grown-up, like someone who could do things and wasn't "just a kid." My mom put something on bee stings, I remembered, but I didn't quite know what. Maybe flour? Some kind of powder that was up in the cabinet. I knew, then, that I'd have to ask my mother when we got back, and that would have only solidified my kid status in Carrie's mind, so I dropped down in the grass next to her.

"I'm okay," she said. "Isn't it sad that he died? They die after they sting you, right? I don't know where he went. I just hit at him to get him off my foot, and he flew over there, somewhere." She motioned to the high grass on her right, and I thought about going over to look, but I knew that even if I found the bee, it would likely be dead, and that would have made Carrie sadder. "I didn't mean to."

"He's probably fine," I said. What I started to say was that it was just a dumb bug—that's what Ben would have said—but I stopped myself. "Want me to look at it?"

Carrie smiled and wiped the tears from her face. "I'm really fine, Joshy. You're a sweetie. Will you promise to stay that way?"

"What? A sweet little kid?" Carrie poked her bottom lip out and reached over to me. She put her hand in my hair but didn't ruffle it like I thought she might. She just put it there, touched my scalp where almost no one else ever did.

"Don't be silly. Listen, tonight's our last night. I want it to be really special, okay? Will you do something for me?"

"Sure," I said. I expected her to propose some plan for Ben, something to make their last night together the best, but instead she asked me to meet her.

"At the pier, after the fireworks your parents brought, okay? I just want to sit there for a few minutes, and I want to do it with you. Can you get away?" Carrie hadn't been back to the lake since that first day. It had been a constant irritation to Ben, who wanted to swim with her and touch her in her blue swimsuit, but she refused. She'd sit on the bank, far from the water and watch us, but wouldn't come back down on the pier.

"Sure," I said again. What could she have asked me, then, that I wouldn't have done?

All day I waited. I watched Carrie and Ben leave on one last walk as I helped my mom clean up the cabin. I packed my things, and then packed Ben's too because I wanted something to do while I waited. Carrie's clothes were everywhere, and I thought briefly about picking them up, but changed my mind. Touching her shirts, her hooded sweatshirt, could be like touching her and I didn't think she'd want me to. Besides, I liked seeing those things lying around, like little pieces of her, discarded but waiting.

When they came back, I was sitting on the porch, reading a comic book I'd brought from home. I'd actually brought several, but hadn't read them much, mostly because Ben wasn't reading them, and if he wasn't, I figured I shouldn't either. As they strolled through the yard, I noticed then how much he'd changed this summer. He was still all arms and legs, but he'd "filled out" as my grandma would say. He wasn't so thin, and he was tanned a dark golden brown. And I could see myself in him—we had the same eyes, the same mess of curly hair. Seeing him turn into a good-looking person gave me hope that one day I might be okay for girls like Carrie to look at too.

"Hey, kid," Ben said, and plucked the comic out of my hand. "Is this mine?"

"No," I said and snatched it back. "It's mine. Jerkwad."

"Asshat," he said and flicked my ear. It hurt, but I smiled because this was the old Ben, harassing me and in a good mood.

"I packed up your stuff," I said. "You weren't going to do it."

"Thanks, Joshy. You're swell." He gave me a hug around the neck that was more of a headlock and rubbed a hard noogie on the top of my head.

"Did you do mine?" Carrie asked. She looked somehow even paler than usual and sounded distracted.

"No, but I can if you want me to," I said, too quickly.

"Oh, I can do it if you want me to," Ben mocked me in a high-pitched girl's voice, then made kissing noises toward Carrie. "Please, let me be your slave."

"Shut up," I said, feeling my face and ears grow hot.

"You wouldn't turn so red if it wasn't true," Ben said, and slugged me hard on the arm, harder than usual, so hard that tears jumped to my eyes.

"Leave him be," Carrie said. Ben stopped smiling and shot her a slant-eyed look.

"Well, maybe you want him to be your slave, huh, Carrie? Your tiny little baby boyfriend."

"I can pick up my own stuff, that's all I'm saying." She tried to squeeze past him and into the cabin, but he grabbed her arm and pulled her back toward him. "Let go," she said. Ben's face softened, and he nuzzled into her cheek.

"Don't be mad. I was just messing with the kid. We do it all the time. That's how brothers are. Right Joshy?"

"Right," I said, but my arm was still throbbing, and a sob rose in my throat. I jumped up from my seat and darted from the porch. I ran toward the lake, not looking back, only thinking about jumping in the Coffin water, which I did, with all of my clothes on. I dove down as far as I could, down until my lungs burned like my shoulder did.

We built a fire that night for the last time, and put hot dogs and marshmallows on long sticks to roast. My hot dog, as usual, fell into the fire. Ben laughed and said something nasty about my burnt wiener. I didn't care, because I knew later I would meet Carrie at the pier.

My parents always bought some fireworks from one of the roadside stands that popped up around the end of June. There were jumping jacks that flew up off the ground before twirling around and quickly dying in the grass. There were fountains that sprayed colored sparks. My favorites were the Roman candles that shot out of a tube and crackled brightly in the air. That, I think, was the thing that nearly blew off that neighbor boy's hand, so only my father was allowed to hold the Roman-candle tube, and my mother was standing by with a bucket of water in case any stray spark started a fire. Ben and Carrie made hearts with sparklers, the after image burning in the air as they kissed. I took handfuls of snappers in their little white bags and popped them against Ben's sneaker. He ignored me until one missed his shoe and popped against his bare ankle instead. He screamed and started chasing me, laughing, around the yard. It was one of those nights that seemed made for memory.

Carrie slipped away when Ben went inside to change out of his shorts and into long pants. The night had gotten cool and damp. I waited a few seconds, then followed her. When I got there, she was already sitting Indian-style on the end of the pier. I pushed off my shoes and sat next to her, dangling my feet into the lake.

The moon was nearly full and cast an eerie light over the lake and onto Carrie's face. She was staring out over the water and didn't turn to me when I sat down.

"Josh," she said.

"Yeah?"

"Thanks for coming out here with me."

"You're welcome. You ain't scared of the lake anymore?"

"I never was scared of the lake," she said. She scooted around so that she was facing me and motioned for me to do the same. Finally we were sitting knee to knee. In the humid air, our skin stuck together like suction cups.

"You're a sweet kid," she said, and put her hands over on my knees. My heart made a sick drop and then leaped up into my throat. I swallowed hard and wiped my sweating palms on my shorts. "I wish I could keep you, and this place, forever."

"You can keep me," I croaked out. I felt like I had never said a truer thing in my life. Carrie smiled and pinched my leg a little.

"I love your brother, you know? Maybe someday we'll all be family. Wouldn't that be awesome?"

I shrugged and looked away from her. My brother did not deserve her love. I was only a kid, but I knew it.

"Oh, Joshy. You'll go to school next year, and you'll find some cute little girl who isn't a complete and utter disaster."

"You're perfect!" I blurted. Why had she asked me out there? It felt like she wanted to twist the knife she'd plunged deep into my heart the first time she'd called me a kid.

"Perfect. Yep, that's me," she laughed and pulled her hands back from my knees. "You have no idea—" I don't know what came over me then. It was as though the pressure that had been building up in my chest, in my head, since the beginning of the week finally made me crazy. I lunged at Carrie, grabbed her around the shoulders and kissed her hard on the mouth. I suppose she was too surprised to move at first, and my teeth smashed against her lip. I tasted blood, and I wasn't sure if it was hers or mine, until she finally pushed me away.

"Shit, Josh! You busted my lip!" Carrie said and patted at the spot on her lower lip with a fingertip.

"I'm sorry," I mumbled, horrified at what I'd done. I put my head down into my hands, humiliated. There was no pleasure in that kiss; only pain and embarrassment.

"Silly," Carrie said, and pulled my hands away from my face. "I would have kissed you if you'd asked."

"You hate me now." The sobs were rising, and I knew I was about to cry like the baby I was.

"How could I hate you?" Carrie said, her face so close to me that I could smell the sweetness of her breath. "You're perfect." It was like a dream, Carrie's face close to mine, and then her lips, soft and wet and a little slippery from the blood touching my lips. I had apparently also busted my own lip from that first disastrous attempt because the pressure from Carrie's mouth made my lips burn and pulse. I could not believe what was happening. It was a perfect thing, and Carrie and I, for that moment, were two perfect people. I shut my eyes and reached for her.

When Carrie's lips were ripped away, I opened my eyes and expected to see her laughing at me or looking sad that I was so young and dumb. Instead, I saw her flying up and back, Ben behind her. He was yanking her to her feet by a handful of her hair.

"What the fuck are you doing?" he screamed. Carrie thrashed around, trying to get out of his grip. "What are you doing to my little brother?"

"Let me go, Ben!" Carrie said, and he did, so quickly that she fell back down onto the dock, now bobbing and swaying from all the weight and movement.

I stood up, maybe to help her or maybe to stand between her and Ben, I wasn't sure.

"Ben—" I started.

"Get back to the cabin," he said, no longer shouting, but staring down at Carrie with that calm, intense stare, that one I knew not to try and argue with. "Go on."

I don't know why I went. Maybe it was because I was scared of Ben. That would be the best story, wouldn't it? That I was afraid he'd hurt me? But I don't know if that's it, or at least if that's the only reason. He was my older brother. I loved him, and I feared him, and I respected him, and I hated him. I always would. And I was confused. I didn't know what else to do, so I went back to the cabin. I didn't look back. I didn't hear the splash of someone falling off the dock into the Coffin water. I didn't see Carrie's arms thrashing as she tried to stay afloat, or Ben standing at the end of the dock, his arms crossed as though he'd made an important decision. I didn't, I didn't, I didn't, I never did.

A blonde girl sits on the edge of the dock, her legs swinging and feet kicking at the water. She's wearing a blue bathing suit, and her skin is so pale that she nearly glows. She is eight, but small for her age. She is mine.

Her older brother is in the water, paddling around and trying to convince her to come in.

"Come on, Margo," he says, and makes a grab for her ankle. "I won't let you drown."

"Daddy said that it's Coffin water," I hear her say. I shout out to Brian to leave her alone, that she'll get in when she's ready, and go back to the lawn chair I'd been sitting in to watch them. There is an open beer there, a novel, and my cell phone. My wife is up at the cabin, making sandwiches and a summer salad. I promised the kids that later we'd build a bonfire. This is the first time I've been back to Teeters Lodge since I was thirteen.

This has been one of the driest summers in anyone's memory. There were stories in the news every day about receding water levels. Just last week, I read about a lake in Michigan that was lower this year than any time in history, so low that the top of a car that had been driven into the lake in 1965 became visible. Recovery crews came in and found four skeletons, still sitting in the same seats they'd been in nearly fifty years. That night, I searched for Teeters on the internet, and found that nothing much had changed except their rental rates. The fact that they had a vacancy on Fourth of July weekend seemed like fate.

The phone rings five times before Ben's wife picks up. "Hey sweetie!" she says when she hears my voice. I picture Lori on the other end, redheaded and big-boned. I can hear the smile. She is Ben's third wife, my favorite so far.

"Hey Lori," I say. "Can I talk to my brother?"

"He's down in the man cave, so it'll take a minute. When are you guys going to come and visit us? I miss those kiddos!"

"Soon, maybe," I say, though it's a lie. I see my brother once, maybe twice a year, and usually at my parents'. I haven't been to Ben's house for two years, since the time I'd seen a bracelet of bruises on Lori's wrist and a tenseness in her smile that I recognized.

"Hey little Joshy," Ben says when he finally gets to the phone. "Long time no see."

"Guess where I am," I say. There is a silence that tells me he guesses correctly, as I knew he would.

"Tell them kids not to drink the Coffin water," he says. "What are you doing there, Josh?"

"You know," I say. "Just checking things out."

I don't know why they didn't look harder for Carrie. The morning after the Fourth of July, her things were gone. My parents, Ben, and I searched the woods. We went to the overlook and asked at all of the neighboring cabins. I never mentioned the fight at the dock; I never asked Ben what happened after I left. I knew that I couldn't. There was nothing I could do. I was just a kid.

Finally, my dad called Carrie's parents, and then called the police. They asked a lot of questions. I heard Ben telling them that Carrie had been acting weird the day before, and I told them that she said she didn't want to go home. It wasn't a lie, not really, but it felt like a betrayal anyway.

It turned out that Carrie hadn't been lying either, when she told me that I didn't really know her. She'd had a lot of trouble at home and had even run away a couple times. It was easy for everyone to believe that she'd done it again, but better. For a while there were even reports of people seeing her in the town closest to Teeters, back home, even as far as Las Vegas or New York. Carrie was everywhere and nowhere.

Ben didn't talk to me about that night, and I never asked. As far as I know, he never said her name again. It was as though once she was gone, he put everything about her in a drawer, and once that drawer was shut, he didn't open it or think about it again. I did, though. I thought about her all the time, every day. I felt the burn on my lips when she kissed me, and the look on her face when the bumblebee stung the bottom of her foot. When I saw Ben's next girlfriend jump out of a still moving car to get away from him, I thought of Carrie. When his first wife filed divorce papers and claimed that he hit her, when no one in my family believed her. When Ben called my wife a bitch at his second wedding reception, then apologized to her with roses and tickets to see her favorite band. When Ben held my baby Margo and his big hand covered her tiny, new head, his fingers gently brushing the soft spot, I thought of Carrie. She's always reminding me of what I could have done for her, but didn't, and what I could have stopped, but wouldn't. Carrie has haunted me, all my life.

"Is it just like you remembered?" Ben asks.

"More or less," I say. "There's new furniture in the cabin, but I kind of miss that old brown chair." I watch as Margo stands up. Brian has floated farther out in the lake, and I can tell that he is waiting for her. She turns and walks back toward the shore, and I think that she's given up, will not swim in Coffin Lake.

"What do you expect to find there, Joshy?" Ben says, just as Margo turns, and I realize what she's going to do. I stand up. She is running, and I start to scream, to tell her to stop, but she is a streak of blond and blue. She is running faster than is possible and is running in slow motion. She is leaving a trail of ghost girls behind her. I blink, but the girls are still there, pale and wearing blue swimsuits, girls that were afraid to jump into the water. Margo is jumping. She is a cannonball. Her brother is waiting there to catch her, or to push her down. "What are you looking for?" Ben asks.

Margo pops up, and Brian grabs her. They are squealing and splashing, celebrating the tiny girl's courage. If she was ever lost, I would never stop looking for her. I would never stop.

"I have to go," I say, and then I am running too. I am diving. My clothes are heavy, but they do not pull me down.

Home Visit

———

Kate parked the car in front of her last home visit—a single-wide trailer tucked into woods so dense that just a little patch had been cleared in the trees for the home and a small yard. It looked shady, cool. She hated to get out into the sticky air, but wanted to get this over with, get home to ice cubes and a circulating fan. She quickly looked at her class roster to remind herself of names. The parents always expected that she would remember their kid from kindergarten registration or the Popsicle social in July, the day all the incoming kindergartners came in to tour the school, play on the playground, and eat frozen flavored ice on a stick. That's what a good teacher would do. She'd been teaching just long enough now to realize it was always going to be like this. Repetition, year after year, faces and names all blurring together. A is for apple; Indian costumes out of paper bags at Thanksgiving; the gift of Christmas ornaments year after year proclaiming her to be the "World's Best Teacher."

The World's Best Teacher wouldn't be so bored today, so ready to throw in the towel, just because of a little heat. She'd already made five visits—the last two belonged to a screamer and an interrupter, respectively—and it was so goddamn hot. She'd also been dealing with Ryan all day, who called every forty-five minutes to make sure she was still alive. He hadn't liked that she was doing this alone. Going to the nice houses close to town was one thing, but when he found out where some of her students lived, he'd gotten nervous. He wasn't from here, didn't know that sometimes it was the ones in the nice houses you had to be most careful of.

The trailer was in a pretty place, down a long dirt drive and close to Green's Run that fed back into the river. She'd lost her cell signal and was glad.

There was a little porch built on the front of the trailer and the yard was freshly cut—probably for her visit. People went to a lot of trouble for her. The few outside toys were collected near an aluminum swing set and a tire swing hung from one of the big trees. It reminded Kate of where she grew up in the next county over. Before she even got out of the car, she knew what it would be like inside, long rooms that always looked a little cramped, a little too full of stuff. Trailers looked lived in, almost immediately, and she'd realized recently as she watched her father patch and mend and replace that they weren't really meant for a lifetime. It was as if they had an expiration date and after too many years, things go wrong and fall apart. Sinks leak into the towel cabinets underneath; floors that had somehow gotten wet need fixing before a foot went through the soft spot. Ceilings grow round brown circles. But still they were good homes.

She picked up her cell phone from the passenger's seat, but before putting it in her bag she saw the "missed call" message and knew there'd be a voice mail from Ryan. She'd explained how important these home visits were in building good relationships with the kids and their families, how necessary to get the parents involved. And they were required by the county. The other teachers already were unsure of her because she was fairly new and young (and a little cautious of her because Ryan was the pharmacist who filled all of their private prescriptions). It wouldn't do her any good to let them think she was afraid of her students or their parents. Besides, today was the only day she'd have to go alone. Her aide, Miss Jennings, would soon be back from her sister's wedding in Wheeling, and they would finish the rest of the class together.

Kate knew how to handle Ryan. It wasn't really so different than getting her students to do what she wanted.

"But Miss Cartwright, I don't want to take a nap today."

"I understand, Pauline, but naps are good for us and, besides, it's only for a little while."

"But Miss Cartwright, Tommy took the green crayon and I need the green crayon."

"I understand, Brian, but it's important to share. Besides, the yellow crayon is just as nice and yellow is my favorite color."

"But Kate, it's not safe, you going all those places alone. Out in the woods, in the middle of nowhere. You don't know those people." Kate hadn't rolled her eyes, though she'd wanted to.

"I understand, Ryan. And it's sweet that you're worried, but this is an important part of my job and sometimes we have to do things we don't necessarily want to do. Besides, I'll be fine and it's only one day."

"But—"

"You can call me," she said. "And I'll call you, okay?" She'd done everything short of offering him a cookie and patting his hand.

The little diamond sparkled on her left ring finger. It was just two months old; a baby, really, in the world of jewelry, but already it seemed like a permanent part of her. Sometimes she'd push it around so the diamond was on the underneath and it looked like a wedding band. The image made her stomach cramp. She tried it once a day, just to see if the feeling was starting to go away. Today it had been the worst yet and she'd thought about tossing the ring out the window and into the thick tangle of underbrush near her car.

She was supposed to be excited about doing this marriage thing, the wife thing, then the baby thing. Everyone around her was getting married. Her high-school boyfriend, Scott Anderson, had not long before married a girl named Rhonda Hoover who did hair at the Sit and Set, the beauty shop where Kate's mother got her hair done. Her mother had just told her that Rhonda was pregnant and that "her belly's so big she can't barely reach my head when she stands back behind that chair." Kate's mother was probably exaggerating, but she could picture it: Rhonda who'd always been tiny, now with a belly that reached out farther than her outstretched arms. Kate knew it'd been her mother's way of hinting that she'd like to see Kate that way, that it was about time for a grandbaby, but Kate had no intention of having kids anytime soon, if ever, and when Ryan brought up the subject, she'd find a way to change it.

Kate'd known Scott since they were kids and when they got together, it seemed natural. That was the thing about where she was from, you knew people forever. The boy who kissed you so hard your teeth ached was the same boy who threw up at the first grade Christmas party and ruined the gift exchange presents. The boy who took you to prom and later hung your plain white underpants on his rearview mirror, he was the same kid who cried when the class mouse died in the third grade.

There was a different kind of trust when you knew things like that about people, when you saw them as kids. There was no way to get that when you met someone in college, like how she met Ryan. Sure, she could visit his parents, see pictures of him as a little boy, but somehow it wasn't enough. Ryan didn't understand, even when she tried to explain to him how she felt like she didn't really know him. "What are you talking about Kate? You know me. We live together. You know me better than anyone." He always thought it had something to do with insecurity, that she didn't trust him or thought he was cheating, but that wasn't it. It was something deeper that she couldn't explain or even name, but she couldn't get around the feeling that something important was missing. She couldn't help thinking about Scott Anderson.

This visit belonged to Henry Rusnak, who she vaguely remembered from the Popsicle social. She only vaguely remembered anything from that day because of Ryan, whom she'd brought along for the first time as her fiancé. At first, she'd liked the approving smiles from the other teachers. They all appreciated how he tried to help, how he volunteered to hand out popsicles to the kids in Kate's class and then stood around talking with a few of the fathers. But then he wandered off, sat alone at a picnic table, and fiddled with his cell phone. He made a call, text-messaged, then played some game. She was so preoccupied watching him that she hadn't paid any attention to the kids or the parents.

Afterward, in the car, she'd told him, "You didn't even try. Couldn't you have been a little bit friendlier?"

"I don't know what you want from me, Kate," he said, driving in that relaxed way with one hand on the steering wheel and the other out the window. She'd always found men driving to be sexy, their confident attention to both the road and to her as she sat in the passenger's seat, but he was irritating her irrationally and she wanted to scream at him to put both hands on the goddamn wheel. What she really wanted was to give him detention for his behavior.

"At least I didn't ask Mrs. Hershowitz how her husband's erectile dysfunction was coming along. Has she seemed any happier to you?" Ryan laughed and Kate thought for the first time about throwing the engagement ring out, into the cornfield they were passing, but she didn't, that day or this one. She twisted the diamond back to the front of her hand and pushed out into the hot, heavy air.

The door creaked open a bit and Henry's head and shoulders emerged. She willed her feet to move.

"Hi, Henry. I'm Miss Cartwright." Henry stared but didn't open the door any wider. He was cute, chilly blue eyes and blond, blond hair almost white from the sun. "Do you remember me?" He nodded but didn't make a move and didn't smile.

"Henry James," a male voice, not deep, a little boyish, said from inside. "Open that door and let your teacher in."

Henry pushed the screen door a little toward Kate and then stepped back.

"Thank you, Henry," she said. "You've grown since the Popsicle social. Have you had a good summer?" Henry shrugged. She had him pegged already. A sulker. Didn't want to come to school because he'd rather be out thrashing through the woods, or playing video games, or maybe riding a four-wheeler. He'd come around though. These were the boys who usually liked to hug her by the end of the year.

"Hi, there," the voice said again. Henry's father came around the bar that separated the living room from the kitchen, wiping his hands on his jeans. He wasn't a tall man, but slim, with the same shock of white-blond hair and blue eyes as Henry. He was wearing jeans and a tucked-in T-shirt, a brown leather belt and work boots, even in summer, even inside. He was so familiar to Kate that she could have named him; he was every boy she'd gone to high school with, every teenage crush she'd ever had, every hometown boy she'd dated.

"I'm Henry's dad, Jeremy," he said and held out his hand to her.

"Of course." Of course his name was Jeremy. It could have just as easily been Brian or Scott or Patrick. Those were the names of the boys in her class, the multiples who had to be Scott A. or Patrick W., depending on their last name. Jeremy was the most popular, though— four in her class alone. For girls it was Kelly or Kerry or Amanda. It wasn't like that anymore. People were looking for "original" names. Last year she'd had an unfortunate child named Tequila Sunrise who looked mean, as mean as a kindergartner could look, and only wanted to use the brown crayon to make art.

She took this Jeremy's hand and was surprised at how cool it was; the trailer was buzzing with the sound of a window air conditioner but was still warm, and Kate felt heated from the inside out.

"I'm sorry I didn't get to meet you at that Popsicle thing they had out at the school." He motioned for her to sit in the recliner. He himself sat on the sofa—brown, maroon flower pattern—and Henry dropped down next to him, crossed his arms, and put his muddy tennis shoes up on the coffee table. Jeremy shot the boy a warning look, and Henry dropped his feet.

"I had to work, so Henry's grandparents brought him out. They help us a lot, don't they, buddy?" Jeremy put his hand down deep into Henry's hair and pushed it around a little. Henry just continued to scowl at Kate, his eyes a million years old, like they could see right through her.

"And where is it you work?" she asked. Being nosey was the biggest reason for doing these home visits—get in, dig as much dirt as you can, get out before they even knew what hit them. A chance to figure out something about the kid before he was sitting in her classroom every day, eating paste or pinching the girl in front of him.

She asked about the job, but what she really wanted to know was where was the Amanda or Kelly of this house. Where was Henry's mom?

"I work over at the lumberyard right now, but I'm taking night classes to get my electrician's license. Henry and I don't get too awful much time together, but hopefully that'll change real soon, when I get done with the classes and all. I'll be here when he gets home from school, for a couple hours, so I'll be able to help him with his homework some and his grandma can help him with the rest."

"Your parents watch Henry then? When you're at work?" Jeremy nodded. "You'll want to make sure to note that on Henry's emergency form, so that if he gets sick in school, we'll have the right number to call." That was a good teacherly thing to say. "I have all that paperwork here for you."

"Oh, sure."

"First, I'd like to go over some school rules, Henry, if that's okay?" She did the program, went through the classroom policies, which she would spend most of the first two or three weeks of class repeating, over and over. She quickly mentioned the schedule for special classes (art Monday, PE Tuesday, music Wednesday, etc.) and told Henry a few of the things he'd learn before the end of the year. She also made sure to highlight fun things, like the Christmas program and graduation. Nothing impressed Henry. He was one of those spooky kids who knew things, had seen things, and he'd be watching her all year.

"Well, I have a few more items I need to discuss with you, Mr. Rusnak, but Henry can go play if he wants," Kate said.

Jeremy was starting to look weary, maybe overwhelmed.

"Can I go play Xbox, Dad?" Henry asked, really the first thing he'd spoken since the visit started. Kate thought she noticed a slight lisp but couldn't be sure. He'd probably need speech class.

"Sure, buddy, go ahead. Come back out when your teacher is leaving, so you can say goodbye." Henry shot back towards his room. "I'm sorry about how he's acting," Jeremy said. "He's not too happy about starting school. He's a good kid, but he'd rather run the woods with his pap all day."

"Understandable," Kate said and smiled. She felt much better now that the boy was gone and noticed again how good-looking Jeremy was. It wasn't in that slick, conventional way, but in a way that reminded her of outside, of sun on a face. She could guess what he smelled like—some cheapish cologne like Old Spice or Stetson, strong and man. Ryan wore some sort of Calvin Klein stuff that came in a frosted white bottle. She'd almost accidentally sprayed it on herself more than once.

"You're probably wondering about his mom," Jeremy said suddenly, just as Kate was preparing to launch into an uncomfortable discussion about snack days and school supplies. Parents almost always tensed up when money was involved.

"You should know, in case it ever comes up in class. She's not in the picture. Left out of here when Henry was three. She wasn't meant to be a mom, and that's okay. Henry and I do fine and my parents help where they can." Kate nodded. "If the other kids are ever doing anything for their moms, Henry'll just do it for his grandma. He and me, we've already talked about it. He's a smart kid, knows how it is."

"Okay."

"Okay." Now that the hard thing was said, Jeremy looked

more relaxed. "So, snack days? What do we bring, like cupcakes or something?" Kate smiled. They finished talking about the importance of nutritional snacks and other parental responsibilities.

"All right," Kate said, looking at the stack of papers she'd placed on the coffee table between herself and Jeremy and going through her mental checklist. "I think the only thing left to talk about then is the learning activities. There are a few little things—helpful tools—the kindergarten teachers like to give parents so they can help their children at home. Are you open to that?"

"Sure. Of course." Kate fished in her bag and took out the prepared baggies of sight words on index cards and the complementary book—*Little Giraffe's First Day of School*—that the PTA sent for each kid. "Do you mind?" she asked and pointed to the sofa. She took her bag and moved next to him.

"These are the first words Henry will be expected to know," she said, handing him the baggy. "They're the most common words like *the* and *we*. Just go over them with him for a few minutes every night." She then handed him the book and the PTA newsletter for new parents. The PTA also sent along a form for the parents to fill out, asking about interest in attending meetings, availability to volunteer at the school, and questions about heavy equipment or other helpful things the parents might have access to that could beautify their child's school. Brighton Elementary had one of the most aggressive PTAs in the state. They struck parents hard and fast, baited them in with a free book and the promise of spring carnivals, then hit them up with fundraisers, school photos and yearbooks, and requests for backhoes and snowblowers.

Jeremy was looking over the letter. Kate noticed how his eyebrows (light blond like his hair) knitted in toward his nose.

"In addition to starting to read and learning basic math, we'll also be focusing on time and currency," she said, gently taking the letter from his hands. "You can use your own money to help Henry practice recognizing the coins, but we like to have parents make a clock with the child, so that he can hold it and manipulate the hands himself." Kate pulled a paper plate from her bag and handed it to Jeremy. She'd been making these all day with mothers, watching polished nails push brass fasteners through the plate to hold on the flimsy, construction paper hands. This was her first father though, and Jeremy looked perplexed. He turned the plate over and over as if there were directions on the back, or like inspiration was suddenly going to come to him. She smiled and handed him a black permanent marker.

"Put the numbers around the front, just like on a clock face," Kate told him. He painstakingly wrote the numbers in that distinctly male hand. His numbers were thin and shaky, no curly end on the two, no smiley face in the zero of the ten.

Kate was thinking about Scott Anderson. When they were in school, he drove a farm-use truck and she'd often go bumping along the side roads with him, the truck smelling warm and dirty. Sometimes he'd let her drive, even though she was just fifteen and didn't have her license. He'd never take his eyes off her as she drove, telling her to go faster, faster, kicking up the dust, until finally she'd brake hard in the road, tires skidding, leaving them both breathless and laughing. He had a Skoal ring in his back pocket and tasted like minty long cut. All summer they'd run the dirt roads, sometimes talking for hours about everything and anything, sometimes never saying a single word. The future was something indefinable, unimportant. Scott never wanted to hold her back, tie her down. He knew her.

There was something through Jeremy's eyes that reminded her a little of Scott, not so much the way they looked—Scott had brown eyes that crinkled at the corners and Jeremy's were that icy blue—but in how they looked, how they focused in and concentrated, how they looked her right in the eye as she talked to them. "Like this?" Jeremy asked as he tried to manipulate the tiny black strips of construction paper she'd given him for clock hands. He had to first push the brass fastener through the hands and then punch the fastener ends through the center of the plate. It was harder for him to do than the mothers with their thin, nimble fingers. His fingers were big, blunt at the ends.

"Just like that," she said. He tore the second hand a little with the pointy end of the fastener, but she told him that was okay. "Later, you can make one with Henry. I've brought parts for another." Kate placed a paper plate and a baggie with another fastener and hands on the coffee table.

"Are you sure Henry will be able to do this?" Jeremy was now battling the plate, trying to get the hands in the center. Everything was looking bent and messy; the hands were too far off to the right and would have a hard time ever making ten o'clock. "Does this look okay?"

"It looks great," she lied. "And Henry will be fine with it. His fingers are littler. You'll just have to give him direction. Have patience."

"Yeah, I bet you got to have a lot of that in your job. You like it?" Jeremy gave up on the paper-plate clock and tossed it to the stand.

"Sure," she said. "I guess." That didn't sound too World's Best Teacher. Normally she would tell the parents what they wanted to hear, how she loved her job, how she had always wanted to dedicate her life to teaching their little darlings. She wouldn't let the doubt into her voice, or the boredom, or the fear that she was doing everything wrong or backward. But she felt like Jeremy was really asking; that he really wanted to know. "It's not always fun," she said. "I got bit once and still have a scar. Sometimes the kids get frustrating."

"Oh . . . I'm sorry."

"I do love it though," she said. "It's very rewarding, and it's great being the person to introduce the kids to education. That's so important." There, that sounded more World's Best. Maybe Jeremy would appreciate her initial honesty.

"So . . . is there anything else I should know?" Jeremy asked. She'd gone through the program, told him all he needed to know to get Henry ready for the first day of kindergarten—Henry who was somewhere in the back of the trailer shooting zombies or stealing pixilated cars. She'd already spent more time here than she had at the other houses; she'd forgotten about wanting to get home, about Ryan's constant calling. She'd even forgotten the heat since she'd moved over to the couch and was sitting next to Jeremy who did smell like Old Spice and faintly of something mechanical, like fuel or grease.

Kate wanted to tell him about how she dreamed of floods, thick brown water that would pick up a trailer and move it, make it a mobile home after all. It was a recurring dream she'd had since she was a kid. Before, she'd be in the trailer as it floated and bobbed, was swept downstream, and she'd look out the back window before waking up with panic in her heart. Lately though, she'd be standing where a backyard would have been and watch as home got farther and farther away. She'd try to chase it, but her feet wouldn't move, mired down. When she'd look down, she'd see Ryan, naked in the mud, half man and half earth, holding her ankles tight, pulling her down.

She might start by asking Jeremy how close that river was to them. Could it break its banks in a heavy rain? Could the violence of a flash flood push the trailer from its moorings?

She'd tried to talk to Ryan about the dreams, but he didn't really understand. "So, was I trying to help you or kill you?" he'd asked. "Did I have legs or were my legs made of mud, like Swamp Thing? I'm sorry, Kate. I don't get it."

Kate didn't get it either. She could only look at him desperately and hope he could understand something she couldn't say; something that had to do with losing control, being caught up, something to do with losing.

Sometimes she woke up and the bed felt like it was moving, slowly as if in rising water; she'd shake Ryan awake. "It's just a dream, Kate," he'd say, not even opening his eyes. He'd pat her with a thick, sleep-drunk hand and roll over. Here she was, stranded on a bed in the middle of a black flood—of rising water—and he'd turn over. She'd shake him again and he'd swat her hand away. "Christ, Kate. Don't be a child. Go to sleep."

On the worst nights, she'd sit up, her back flat against the headboard and her knees pulled up to her chest until the morning light came through the windows and turned the dirty and deadly black water back into bedroom floor. Then Ryan would wake up, yawn, stretch, and put his feet down as if the room hadn't been a raging flood.

What would Scott or this Jeremy have told her if she'd said the floor had turned to water and she was afraid to get caught in it? He knew her; he'd understand and hold her. He wouldn't tell her that her dream didn't mean anything. He'd say he'd just been having the same one, but in his, the flood waters were receding, and home was coming back.

"Ms. Cartwright?" Jeremy was looking at her, his cool eyes questioning. "Are you okay?" Kate moved closer to him, put her hand on his leg. He looked down at it, confused. Hadn't he realized everything since she walked in the door had been leading toward this? She moved her face closer to his. She wanted to kiss him, to feel his rough lips on hers and remember.

"I don't think that's a good idea," he said. She moved closer to him still, waiting for him to make the move, to meet her. "I think you should go." He backed away, and his voice wasn't kind.

"I—I'm sorry," Kate stammered. She pushed her things into her bag and stood up. She felt stricken, the heat rising back into her, burning. What had she done?

"Me too," he was staring at her, judging, disapproving and disappointed. Kate knew she wasn't the kind of girl he knew, and she sure as hell wasn't the World's Best anything.

Kate fumbled for the doorknob. "I'm sorry. I'm sorry," she said, then mumbled something about the heat, confusion. She got out the door, finally. Maybe she could tell the school that she hadn't been in her right mind. It was some fevered dream that overtook her. She'd thought they both were someone else.

The air felt heavy and the sky had turned gray. She'd get in her car and drive away. Tomorrow, she'd call and talk to the principal. If

Jeremy hadn't already called, she'd make up some lie to get Henry out of her class.

A storm was coming. After all the heat, it would be a big one, a violent release of built-up electricity, and she would be on the road, trying to see through the rain and find her way home. At the top of the long drive, she'd find her phone and call Ryan, Ryan who was trying as best he knew how. She'd call to let him know that she was still alive, but about to be caught in a downpour.

Handlers

---

*J*ill stubbed her toe on Mr. Washuta for the second time that day and cursed under her breath. The cemetery had misaligned his monument some twenty years ago, making the corner of the thick, black marble slab stick out right in the path Jill took every day from her trailer to the mailbox and back. "Dammit Washuta."

Her home was part of Joann Leeds's trailer court, which wasn't really an organized settlement, but just a few old mobile homes thrown on a couple dozen acres of ground. Bobby and Jill had the one with the up-close and personal view of the cemetery because it was the cheapest. The idea of waking up every morning to rows of marble monuments bothered some people, but Jill didn't care.

The trailer was a mess. She'd not felt like washing dishes for three days and the workbooks Bobby had been studying to prepare for the GED lay everywhere.

Jill dropped on the couch next to him and kicked off her shoes. "There were some dark clouds rolling in. Looks like it might rain." His eyes lit up and he raised his eyebrows. "Don't even think about it," she said and shivered a little, remembering the early summer storm she, Bobby, Ellie, and Shep had chased. They did it a lot, following the storm in Shep's Pinto, looking for lightning strikes and funnel clouds, but they'd never seen a tornado. Luckily, the funnel had disappeared nearly as quickly as it had come. Bobby was excited and gave a loud whoop. Ellie laughed nervously and Shep shook his head. Jill got out of the car and puked beer and adrenaline.

"Flip on the base, baby, and let's see if old Shep's got his ears on," Bobby said.

Jill turned the knobs on the huge base CB, keyed the mike, and said, "How 'bout it Mount'n Boy?" For a minute they both listened to the crackle. Finally, "Go ahead."

"You talk," she told Bobby. "I need to grade papers."

"No fun." He rolled over on his stomach and reached for the mike. "Test, one two three, test one two miss mary mac mac mac all dressed in black black black over. How bout'cha Mount'n Boy? This is Red Rover coming at ya." Oh no, Jill thought. So it begins. And on a Wednesday night. Shit.

"Do not get them over here tonight, Bobby," Jill whispered, as if Bobby were on the phone.

"Red Rover Red Rover, tell Poison Ivy to bring her ass on over." That was Ellie, Jill's younger sister. She and Shep had been married for nearly two years. The little sister got married first, a fact their mother never failed to remind Jill of each and every time they were together.

"Ten-four," Bobby said back to Ellie.

"NO," Jill mouthed.

"Er, that's a negative Barefoot Baby. Ivy's given me a glare."

"Well bull-shit! What stick's wandered up her ass?"

"It didn't wander. It was firmly placed there by the Preston County Board of Education."

"Ten-four." Ellie laughed.

Bobby keyed the mike too close to the speaker and made it squeal.

Shep had a decent base and a pretty fancy mobile in the Pinto hooked up to a linear for more power, but Bobby's was crap. The pickup's mobile was duct-taped; the base had been welded twice and started smoking every once in a while. Still, it was a step up. Before he found the base at a flea market, Bobby had only had an old mobile for inside. He'd had to carry a car battery into the trailer to run it. The battery had sat in a box in the living room for two months.

Radio static erupted again and it was Shep, practically yelling.

"Well, you just tell that gal we'll be there directly. Help remove that stick."

"Shit," Jill said and threw the red pen she'd been holding.

"Ten-four. Over and out." Bobby shrugged.

"Why didn't you tell them not to come? I told you I had stuff to do and I have to get up early in the morning."

"You tell them. She's your sister."

"Hell. I'm going to the bedroom to grade these essays. Could you leave me alone for a while so I can get them done? Please?"

"I wasn't bothering you, baby." She grabbed an apple off the table and threw it at him. He caught it, laughed, and took a bite.

Jill wanted to be mad, but she was too tired. It wasn't that she wouldn't like to get loud and drunk with Ellie and sing off-key as they tore up the dirt roads, but things were different now and changing all the time. It was one thing when she was only subbing, but now she had a permanent place as a tenth-grade English teacher. She'd tried a few days of hungover sentence diagramming, smelling like stale beer and cigarette smoke. When she told Ellie how it felt, how it was seeing her students with blurry eyes and hearing their questions as if in a tunnel, Ellie laughed and said she bet none of them even noticed. Jill wanted to believe that, but knew they had. She was young, and looked even younger, and that didn't make discipline easy. Ellie didn't understand. She liked the job. She didn't want to screw this up and knew they couldn't afford to.

She got through two papers. Her students were writing about *Romeo and Juliet*, which they'd labored through for over two weeks. It made her sick to realize how little they understood, even after all that time. The first essay was a terribly written one about how parents screw up their kids and the other was by a girl raised by brutally religious parents—her thesis revolved around the statement: "If only they had embraced God earlier . . ."

In the front room, Bobby turned on the radio and found a country station. Dolly Parton was singing about Jolene. Jill pushed the papers off her lap and lay back onto the bed.

She'd shut her eyes for just a minute before she heard the door slide open and felt Bobby's weight on the bed. Before she'd fallen asleep, she'd been thinking about the time she and Ellie had stayed up all night, long after Bobby had gone to bed and Shep had passed out on the sofa. She'd been drinking some creation of Ellie's that consisted of a dash of Captain Morgan, some vodka, and something else, all mixed with orange pop. She'd known it was a bad idea but did it anyway. She and Ellie gave each other aliases, Peanut Butter and Dixie Cup, and spent hours teasing truckers on the CB. In sexy voices, they promised home-cooked breakfasts to lonely drivers. Jill liked to think she sounded innocent, meant only breakfast, while Ellie was overt and scandalous, but she knew the implications were the same.

Either way, it didn't matter. They'd given false directions and sent the poor fools to Hardees looking for a red Cutlass, then to the Qwik Mart for a green sedan. When they were found out or the trucker lost interest, they switched stations and started over again, "How 'bout any late-night drivers out there wantin' to talk to two pretty ladies? Any big rigs out there tonight?" Dixie Cup had an accent that sounded like a mixture of Scarlett O'Hara and Elly May Clampett.

"You okay? What's up?" Bobby was on his stomach next to her; she felt his voice in her ear.

"I'm okay," she said without opening her eyes. "I'm just tired." She didn't tell him her dad had driven her to the doctor the day before while Bobby was at work. While Bobby'd been pumping gas or checking oil, she'd been sitting on cold metal, wearing a paper dress.

"Shep and Ellie are just around the bend. He just hollered. They stopped for beer at The Market and'll be here in five."

"Great." Jill groaned and put her arm across her eyes. "You're screwing up my essays," she said half-heartedly. She didn't really care if he crinkled them all, if he destroyed them. They were shit anyway. No one cared about Shakespeare today, including her.

She stepped onto the porch just in time to see Shep's dark-orange Pinto come tearing through the cemetery. Bobby had already opened the gate because Shep seldom slowed down to look. He'd crashed it twice already. The tall CB antenna stuck out on top like a weather vane and bounced as the car fell into ruts. Every other day Shep knocked the magnetic antenna down, going too fast under the low land bridge in Morgantown when he picked Ellie up from the university.

The car radio was loud, screaming "Bad Moon Rising" out into the cloudy evening. Ellie was half-hanging out the window, waving a can of beer and singing "there's a bathroom on the right" at the top of her lungs, even though Jill had told her the right lyrics at least a dozen times.

Shep hit the brakes hard, making gravel fly and the can go sailing out of Ellie's hand. It rolled backward, the gravel popping holes, streams of Coors Silver Bullet shooting out. Bobby, Shep, and Ellie all howled.

"Look at you, look at you!" Ellie fluffed the ends of Jill's newly cut and rolled under hair. "Don't you look old."

"You think?" Jill asked. "Bobby hates it."

"That's because you look all grown-up." Ellie smiled and threw her arm around Jill's shoulder. Jill envied her sister's long, wild hair, her slim hips, her cutoffs and T-shirt. Jill looked down at herself and saw loose sweatpants and flip-flops. Put her hand up and felt her old lady's hair. She wanted to cry. "So what are we gonna do tonight? Shep got a new thingy-ma-doodle for the base so they're gonna be busy for a while." Jill looked over to where Bobby and Shep were crouched on the floor, hovering over the base.

"What is it?" Jill asked.

"Who the hell knows." Ellie had emptied a Coors into a tall glass and was adding in a crazy straw.

"I'm not drinking tonight," Jill said. She spoke softly then felt stupid for feeling so guilty. "I have school tomorrow."

"Well I do too!" Ellie said, meaning her one communications class at 2:30 p.m. "Oh, come on Jill. Don't be such a prude." Ellie pushed herself up on the countertop and swung her feet into the cupboard doors. The *thrump, thrump* suddenly made Jill furious.

"Stop!" She yelled, and everyone did, including Shep and Bobby, who stared at her. "You're such a child, Ellie." Jill felt her face turning red. If she had something in her hand, she would have thrown it. There was silence around her. The only noise was the static and squawk coming from the CB.

"Goddamn, Jill. What the hell?" Ellie hopped down from the counter and slammed down her glass.

"Hey, hey, girls, no reason to fight," Shep was up and draped his arm over Ellie's shoulder. He knew her temper, wanted to diffuse the situation before she got out of control.

"Yeah, come on," Bobby got up from the floor and started to the door. "It's too damn hot in here. Let's get out. Let's go run around. Come on Jill. You can drive." Jill didn't usually drive and Bobby only wanted her to when he wanted to concentrate on drinking and causing trouble. The last time she'd driven was when they were coming home from Morgantown, when Shep had hooked up the siren, put the red light on the dash and switched the CB mike from broadcast to amplify. They all thought it was hilarious when the cars along Route 7 would pull over, expecting an ambulance or police car and all they'd see was a rickety Pinto blowing by. They'd put Jill behind the wheel because that'd be so much funnier, this serious looking blonde on her way to some emergency.

"Okay, but no shit," Jill said as she took the keys from Shep. "Shep, you promise, no shit?"

"Why sure," Shep kissed her loud and sloppily on the cheek before whooping and heading out the door.

"I'm serious!" she shouted as Bobby and Ellie pushed out of the trailer and into the darkening night. As Jill pulled the door shut behind her and started down the makeshift wooden steps, the first drop of rain plopped on her nose and a roll of thunder echoed in the distance.

"It's gonna be a good one," Bobby said, folding his tall frame and squeezing into the back of the Pinto. Shep was already back there and Ellie was waiting in the passenger's seat. "Come on baby."

Ellie was jabbering on and on about two girls in her biology class who squealed when the fetal pig in a jar made its rounds. Ellie hated fakes.

Bobby and Shep had the CB mike stretched into the back and Bobby kept reaching his long arm up past the console, changing stations as they looked for someone familiar to talk to or harass.

It was raining heavier and the windshield wipers swished back and forth, squeaking in the middle. It was darker and darker, so she switched on the headlights and watched the beams light up the rain. The radio was playing and she was thinking of her dad. When they went running around with him, the radio was never turned on. He would sing and he always drove. Slowly and erratically to the rhythm of the song. Hank Williams called for slow and swerving; sometimes Ernest Tubb or Tennessee Ernie Ford would pick it up. He was always singing, but only drove to tempo when he was drinking and running the dirt roads. He hadn't said a word when she called and asked him to drive her to the doctor after school. He hadn't asked about Bobby. He just came over and got her, waited in the car while she was inside, then silently drove her home.

Ellie was still talking, now about a boy she knew in elementary school who she was sure was beaten by his father. Talking about the past meant she was getting drunker. "The things people do to their kids. Do you remember him Jillie? He was the tiniest thing I ever saw.

Littler even than me. And those bruises. Don't you remember? They looked like clouds. I never want kids. Screw it." She'd lit a cigarette and out of the corner of her eye, Jill was watching the little red ball of fire swerve around in the dark like a sparkler, but it wasn't bright enough to write a magic name, the shadow lasting for a second and then disappearing. Jill wished that she had an Independence Day sparkler now. She'd write something crazy. Not her name. Maybe Peanut Butter or Dixie Cup. Maybe Poison Ivy.

"Gotta piss babe," Bobby said and tapped her head rest. Jill pulled over on the side of the road, listening as the tires crunched the loose gravel. No cars were coming, no houses on this stretch of old dirt road and not much traffic even in the sunny daylight. Bobby pushed up the back of the seat, crunching Jill into the steering wheel as he climbed out. She put her head on the wheel, her cheek resting in the soft middle. Shep had found a cross-country truck driver who was promising to send him a QSL when he got back to California. Shep loved collecting cards from other CBers, had a shoebox full under the bed. And he liked sending ones from West Virginia, a cardinal on a snowy branch, a black bear in a green field, a tumbledown barn with Mail Pouch on the side in yellow. He always tried to think of pithy things to write, but usually just settled on "Your friend from the Mountain State, Mount'n Boy. Keep your ear to the squeal and the squelch turned down, good buddy."

Jill listened as Bobby peed, the water hitting the gravel. He hummed.

Ellie was singing terribly off-key. Drunk and loud. "I'm the happiest girl in the whole USA." She waved her arm, broad and sweeping, hitting Jill and sloshing a little beer onto Jill's leg. "Shine on me sunshine," loud into Jill's ear. Shep was laughing that Shep laugh, the one that made him sound shy and sweet, bad and nasty all at the same time. The radio squealed. Someone was keying the mike close to a speaker creating that ear-splitting scream.

Bobby and Shep were busy cussing Town Talk, who'd been

monopolizing the airwaves. They'd been feeling powerful. With the souped-up mobile, they could flip on the linear and splash three channels up and three down with their voices. They liked to hear the others getting frustrated when they couldn't carry on their own conversations, but then Town Talk came on, flipped some switches and blew them off the air.

They hadn't even noticed when Jill steered the Pinto toward home. As she turned into the cemetery and started toward the trailer, the last verse of "American Pie" played and they all stopped talking and sang along. The mellow verse without background music. The sad, haunting one. Even Jill. Their voices were in unison, and for that moment even Ellie sounded on key. The music picked up for that very last chorus. Bobby and Shep sang louder, pounding the headrests with the palms of their hands. Jill stopped the car with a jolt and quickly shut off the ignition.

The rain had stopped, their yard a muddy mess. Jill's flip-flop stuck in a deep puddle. She left it.

The stale, bottled-up heat, trapped inside before the rain and thunder came to soothe it all down, hit Jill in the face when she pushed in the door. Shep went straight to the base. Bobby went to their radio, switched it on, and turned it up loud so that the thumping rhythm nearly made the trailer vibrate. Ellie grabbed the half-empty glass with the crazy straw from the counter where she'd left it earlier and took a drag. It had to be piss warm and flat, but she was too far gone to care.

Jill danced with Bobby in the middle of the floor. Shep was trying to fiddle with the CB but was mostly just blinking at the dials and waiting for Town Talk to unkey his mike. He'd been holding it up to his TV and broadcasting MASH for the past twenty minutes. Ellie stood on the couch, swaying a little, dancing alone.

"You've been weird today," Bobby said, hardly sounding drunk at all. He could do that. Keep his voice steady and unslurred, even when his brain was soggy and nearly pickled.

"Yeah, I know."

"Are you mad? I'm sorry." He buried his face in her hair, nuzzled her neck.

"No," Jill said. "I'm not mad." She pulled him close and held on as tight as her thin arms could. She felt weak and tried harder, squeezing and tensing her muscles. Bobby's grip on her tightened a little, and she appreciated it. How much of this would she have to let go? How much would she lose in the change? She tried again to hold tighter. Maybe some things she could keep.

At a quarter till three Ellie finally curled herself into a ball in the corner of the sofa, pulled the scratchy crocheted afghan over herself, and said "night." Shep eventually gave up and took the other end of the couch. He didn't pass out; he just went to sleep, half-sitting, half-lying with one foot on the coffee table and the other on the floor.

Eventually Bobby went to the bathroom and never came back. When Jill went looking, she found him lying face down on their bed, his clothes still on and his feet hanging off the end.

The CB was nearly silent. Just some occasional cracking, but no voices. Shep had left it on channel 36, their channel.

At three on the dot, the silence was broken, first by the clicking sound of a keyed mike then by Town Talk, signing off: "Time for all good little boys and girls to be in bed," he said. "Good night Ma and goodnight Pa and goodnight Uncle Alice." Then he sang the chorus of James Taylor's "Sweet Baby James." There was almost something beautiful in his arrogance. Something desperate. He thought when he turned off his CB, it was all over. When he went to sleep, all the radio life stopped. He had to make up this story, sing everyone off the radio, because he couldn't stand the thought of that world going on without him.

Jill turned off the CB, watched the lights go out and the little red bouncing needles go back to zero.

She eventually grew tired of listening to the snores and retreated to the porch. She sat there until the sky began to lighten. She put her hand on her belly and wondered if she could feel anything different there. Any little stirring of life or change. In an hour she would go inside. She would peel off her clothes, climb into the steamy shower and wash away the night. Before putting on her teacher clothes and drying her hair, she would stand sideways and look at her body's profile in the mirror. It was too early, she knew, but she could imagine a little bulge there in her middle. A little stretch.

She'd tell Bobby later that day, after going to school and being called a stuck-up bitch by an angry tenth grader. She'd tell Bobby and he'd whoop. He'd swing her around, then run to Murphy's, buy a pink teddy bear and a catcher's mitt. Later she'd confess that she wished they could go back in time and get married so their baby wouldn't someday ask why she was born only seven months after the wedding. Bobby would then try to think up plans for altering the marriage certificate, maybe paying off the justice of the peace or just using a black marker and changing the date himself. In the end they wouldn't do anything and it didn't matter. They'd just jump in the car, grab Shep and Ellie, stop at Montgomery Ward to buy a cheap white dress off the clearance rack and head to Garrett County, Maryland, where blood tests weren't required.

But now Jill sat alone, watching the sky being cut into slits of red and orange and listening to the sounds of sleep coming from inside. She didn't know that in a few years she and Bobby would move to Virginia where he would work in hot asphalt, making paved roads and patching holes while she taught high school to the children of people who worked in the Pentagon. She didn't know that she'd only see Ellie and Shep on holidays, that their kids would grow up strangers, that no one would use CBs anymore except truck drivers or that Shep would throw away his shoebox of QSL cards the day his father died of lung cancer. Jill didn't know how, but she could feel the change coming, rolling in like a thunderstorm. She knew it would happen, for better or worse, things would slip away, things would come, and in some ways no day would ever be better than this.

Love, Off to the Side

———

Mae only packed what she could carry—just one suitcase, a brown grocery bag full of CDs, and an old picture album. All the pictures with Lou, she left. When she was done, she was done and she didn't want some blurry photograph around to remind her.

The suitcase lived in the back of her closet. To pull it out, she had to pass through his shirts that smelled of lemon laundry soap and sometimes cigarettes; she had to tug and tug until it emerged like a stubborn baby into the world. Each time she shoved it into the closet, she hoped it would stay, but she was going, from another man, another house, and another chance to be someone other than that girl who kept doing this.

Lissy was coming. "I'll be there," she said when Mae called, just like the other times. It'd just take a little longer because with Lou, Mae'd moved nearly an hour away, the farthest she'd ever gone.

Lissy'd always gotten it right. She knew to choose men who wouldn't cling or want too much. In high school, she'd liked the older guys, the ones out of school who sometimes worked at the auto-repair shop and had half moons of grease under their fingernails. Lissy would come to Mae's house with black circles and smudges on her skin, fingerprints and evidence of a love too urgent to wait for a handwashing. She picked the guys who would touch and kiss, leave fake bruises instead of real ones.

When Lissy got there, she would have her shotgun behind the bench seat of the old green pickup, but there wouldn't be any trouble. Lou was at work and would be till dark. And even if he weren't, he'd cry before he'd fight, would beg and grovel, be too weak and flimsy for anybody to lean on, just like always. Mae couldn't live with such a doughy-faced boy with fleshy lips and a weak chin.

When Lissy came, she would be playing Bon Jovi, loud. Maybe "Bad Medicine" or "You Give Love a Bad Name." Lissy liked hair bands and power ballads, Poison and Whitesnake. She kept a cassette player in the truck, just so she could pop in the old tapes she'd had since she was thirteen. Sure, she could find the songs on CD, but it wouldn't be the same. It wasn't just the song, but its physical manifestation, the hard plastic and paper label that her fingers had touched hundreds of times, that held the memory.

Mae went to the bathroom and put on red lipstick, pulled a brush through her long, wavy blond hair. Her mother'd always said that her hair was a rat's nest; twice when Mae was young, her mother had taken scissors to it. She had wildly chopped, snipped, great hanks of hair falling to the floor. The first time, Mae'd been in the fifth grade and the other kids laughed and pointed at the boy length, the uneven edges; teachers just looked at her sad.

Every time Mae left, she knew she was proving her mother right. That she was no good. That there were happy endings for some people, but not for her kind. Mae searched for love and held on to any little piece she could find, hoping that it would turn into more, but usually it just ripped off, like fabric that was stretched too tight, and she'd end up alone, with just some sad corner.

Mae touched things as she passed through the little house. She let her hand slide along the back of the ratty sofa where Lou would lay at nights when he came home, tired and sore, but not wanting to go to bed. He worked in the coal mines, like his daddy and all his four brothers, because that's what he knew. He didn't love it or hate it; it's just what he did and that's all. He'd usually come home dirty, smelling of underground and the oil of machinery. Sometimes, at first, she felt so lonely for him during the day, that when he came home, she threw herself into his arms, kissed him without caring. She stripped off her clothes, and he left dirty smudges on her arms, her thighs, her stomach, signs that maybe she was finally getting it right.

The house was tiny, all he could afford, but he liked it. "It makes me feel good," he told her. "I've never had nothing of my own before, but now I've got this house and I've got you." He meant it to sound sweet, but it made Mae's skin get tight. Maybe Lou just meant that he loved her, like his house, and that she was valuable and precious, but Mae started to hate the three little rooms, and the black smudges on her skin started to seem like evidence of someone marking his territory instead of signs of love. Lissy would say, "Don't let some man think he owns you. You let him think that and you're done for."

Mae first met Lou at the Golden Egg, where she was waitressing. She brought him beer in a glass foggy with fingerprints. He was so nervous, even just sitting there, that he reached for the glass too soon and Mae was confused, fumbled, dropped the glass and it spilled all down his front. She expected him to get mad, to call her a dumb bitch, but he just smiled and pushed at the wet with a wadded-up napkin.

Lou was the youngest in his family and Lissy said that accounted for a lot. He was baby-fied, but also always trying to prove himself to his big brothers, all of whom Lissy deemed better men than Lou and one of whom she'd let take her out to his pickup one night at The Egg. Lou, Mae, and Lissy had all gone to The Egg together after work.

"You'll be happy to know that I'll soon be off your couch, Lissy," Mae had said. Lissy was eating salty peanuts and looking bored.

"Why's that?" Lissy did hair at the Sit and Set while saving up to open her own place and when it was slow, she did her own hair, makeup, and nails all day. This night, she had a blood-red manicure and her hair teased up in some retro beehive/ponytail. She sometimes liked to create costumes for herself and no one ever really looked twice. If anyone could wear a beehive in the Golden Egg, it was Lissy.

"Lou's asked me to move in with him." Mae held Lou's hand and he looked proud, like he'd just earned some award. Lissy laughed, mean, like it was a joke.

"What? You're gonna go live with this boy?" Lou's face turned red, but he didn't say a thing.

"Come on, Lissy." Mae heard the pleading sound in her voice, and hated it, but there it was. "It'll be good. I even quit my job so that I don't have to drive so far every day. It's a good thing. Really."

"No, no. It'll last. You two are meant for each other." She was still laughing, looking right into Mae's eyes so she'd know the joke. Mae felt Lou squeeze her hand and when she turned to him, he was smiling, like he believed Lissy. Like he just got some kind of blessing. "Now, if you two crazy kids will excuse me, I need to see that man over there about something he owes me." She pointed toward the bar where Lou's brother Jackson was standing with a group of men. Lissy was welcomed into that group and they all laughed, together.

When they first met, Lissy was ten and Mae was eleven. Lissy's family had just moved up from some place in Kentucky. She was already outgrowing a little girl's body; she had stringy hair black as coal and three chicken-pox scars in a line on her forehead. They were both in the same grade—Lissy started kindergarten when she was four because her birthday was in December. "My mama said all she wanted for Christmas was a pretty little girl," Lissy said in her mountain accent, a little twisted and high; some kids made fun of it, but Mae thought everything about Lissy was beautiful. "Too bad all she got was me."

Over the years, Mae would hear the story again and again, every time Lissy met someone new or was asked her date of birth at a hospital or DMV, but Mae always remembered the first time, on the day they met.

Mae was an awkward girl in long dresses and thick gray socks. All Mae's clothes were miniatures of her mother's, from dress to shoes to the plain cotton underwear. Even at ten, Lissy saw herself as Mae's rescuer and never stopped seeing it that way. First it was bringing her junk food at lunchtime—kids' food like potato chips and soda instead of the leftover meatloaf sandwiches and white milk in a thermos. When they got older, it was bringing extra clothes to school for Mae to change into, lipstick and blush, nail polish in shiny candy apple red. Mae's mother thought Lissy was a bad influence, especially when they got to be teenagers and Lissy got a "reputation," but after what Tommy and Lissy did, Mae's mother left them all alone.

Tommy Benson was the first boy Mae thought she loved and the reason her mother took the scissors to her the second time. Mae'd been keeping her hair down, long, in her face, to hide the purple love bruise on her neck. Tommy called it a monkey bite; Lissy called it a hickey and laughed when she saw the first one. "That's so childish," Lissy said. "Only kids give each other hickies."

First, her mother was just going to pull Mae's hair back, brush it away from her face and into a neat ponytail or bun. She'd told Mae to do it, but then took matters into her own hands. When she saw the mark on Mae's neck, she went to the bathroom sink and got the silver scissors.

"Is this who you are?" she asked, looking at Mae with such disgust, such disappointment. "Is this who you want to be?" Mae wanted to say no, that she wanted to be someone else, but that it was already too late.

After her mother cut her hair, short and jagged and as ugly as she could, Mae sneaked out her window and went to Lissy's.

"It's my own fault," Mae tried to tell Lissy when she saw the fire flash in her eyes. "I should have known better."

Lissy called Tommy then. He never came into the room, never said a word to Mae, just looked at her from the door, squeezing and unsqueezing his hands into fists.

"You stay here," Lissy told Mae as she pulled on her knee-high leather boots. She looked so good in her denim miniskirt and black leather jacket, high boots and red lipstick, she could have been going anywhere.

Mae made herself not see that Lissy first went to the kitchen and got a knife, one from the wooden block with a thick blade made for chopping. Later, Mae would wonder how much that moment when Lissy chose to take the knife had made them all who they were going to be.

When Lissy came back, she draped a towel over Mae's shoulders and fixed the choppy hair as best she could. Then they dyed it red, just for spite.

The next morning, Mae's mother was in the kitchen when Mae came home. She never looked Mae in the eye; her bun was gone. There were two suitcases by the door and at first Mae thought they were for her. Without saying a word, her mother left—took the bags to the car and drove away.

Mae knew she went to her sister's two hours away because her Aunt Linda sent her a check once a month for a while. Her mother paid the bills from there—electric, phone—until Mae was eighteen, but she never spoke to Mae again. When she was done, she was done.

Mae stayed away from the house as much as she could. She worked at McDonald's; she hung out with Lissy and Tommy, but sometimes she had to go home. Some nights she had to be there and was so alone. It was just her and the shame of chasing her mother away. Tommy said the house gave him the creeps, like it was watching him from inside somehow.

For a while, Mae avoided her mother's room. She went through every other, opening drawers, touching old Christmas ornaments in a plastic crate in the attic, sorting through a small box of her baby things. But when all that was done, only her mother's room remained, the door always shut.

Mae was surprised when she finally went in. She didn't know what she'd been expecting, really. Maybe cobwebs hanging from the mirror or eerie music playing; what she found was just a room mostly cleared out of clothes and personal touches, though there was never much of either. Most of the dresser drawers were empty, except for one, the very bottom on the nightstand. There, Mae found her mother's braid, gray and coiled like something that had once been alive.

Mae had assumed that Lissy had taken the hair after cutting it from Mae's mother's head, maybe as some sort of battle trophy or souvenir. Mae had even imagined it curled much the same way in various locations around Lissy's room. Somehow, the fact that Lissy had left it there for Mae's mother seemed even crueler. And now, her mother had left it there for Mae.

When Tommy turned eighteen, he left home and Mae moved with him into a trailer with orange shag carpeting and brown circles on the ceilings from leaks.

Mae still thought of Tommy sometimes, how surprised he looked the first time he hit her, like his hands had a mind of their own. Mae hadn't wanted to leave him, but Lissy wouldn't let her stay. "He'll kill you, Mae. He won't mean it, but he will." She helped Mae pack her things; he just let them leave, watched out the kitchen window, then turned his back as Mae got in Lissy's truck.

That was the first time she went to live with Lissy. She got the job at The Egg to help with rent while Lissy went to the beauty college. When Lissy came home at night, she'd practiced what she learned on Mae. She'd set her hair, pluck her eyebrows, do thick Cleopatra eyes or the subtle "no makeup" makeup. When she was finished, she'd turn Mae to the mirror and say, "Well, what do you think? A new you?" Mae would smile, nod, tell her friend how talented she was, but never felt transformed. Instead, she heard her mother's voice. "Is this who you want to be?"

Mae took the bag of things out to the front porch and propped it up against the coming-to-pieces recliner Lou had put there as a luxury, a place to drink beer and watch the sunset. Once, she'd taken off all her clothes, all except her brown cowboy boots and sat in that chair, one leg thrown over the arm, and waited for him to come home. The look on his face was burned into her mind, how his eyes got big and the whites looked so white next to the black coal dust on his face. "Jesus H., Mae. What the hell?" She let her foot bounce up and down a little, trying to embody some sort of temptress, someone in control, like Lissy, but when Lou pounced on her, it was just to cover her up with his own body and hustle her inside. "What if somebody seen you?"

"No one saw, Lou. We don't have any neighbors. Three cars pass a day." He let go of her as soon as they got inside and she stood in the middle of the living room, feeling silly.

"There are more than three cars, Mae. And we do have neighbors. There are the Petersons, the Crabtrees—"

"I don't care how many fucking neighbors we have, Lou!"

"Just sitting out there like that, in front of God and everybody."

She looked down at herself, at her paleness, at the little red circles on her arms where his fingers had squeezed as he rushed her inside. She felt like a fool. She wished he would just hit her. If a man came home to Lissy sitting naked on his porch, he wouldn't care who saw and he wouldn't push her inside. He'd strip down too and lay on the splintering porch for her.

Before Lou, it was Jake. It had been bad when she left. Lissy had pulled out the shotgun and pointed it at Jake when he grabbed Mae's arm. "Let her go," she said. "And I mean now." Mae had no doubt that Lissy would shoot, and Jake must have thought so too because he let Mae go right then.

"You're making a big mistake, girl," he said, and Mae stopped because he might have been right. But Lissy saved her and told her to get in the truck.

Jake was older, in his forties, and thought Mae would marry him. He gave her a ring, even though she said she didn't want to get married, didn't want to have kids. He just smiled like he knew what she really wanted and shoved the tiny diamond ring down onto her finger. She went right to the bedroom and called Lissy.

After picking her up, Lissy took her to the strip job. It was private property, but no one ever came by to complain. Once, it had been trees and a stream, then it had been stripped down to mounds of dirt and opened up bare so the coal seams could be cleaned out. Now it was "reclaimed," which meant grassy with a few spindly trees that were fighting to hold on in the loose dirt. It was the perfect place to sit in the dark, listen to Journey, and drink cheap beer.

"We got to get that thing off you," Lissy said, eyeing the ring on Mae's finger. It was too small and, though Mae had tried everything, nothing had worked. "I've got something."

Lissy had a bag of tools behind the seat of her truck. When she first pulled out the snips, with the pointy ends looking like some sort of torture device, Mae said no.

"Come on. It'll be okay. I know what I'm doing. I think. Give me your hand." Lissy started from the palm side, using just the small ends to snip at the band until it started to give. Finally, she was able to snip it in two and bend the ends back enough to pull the ring off. "Voila!"

"Damn!" Mae said and shook her hand. Lissy had gotten too close with the cutters and drawn a little red bead of blood on the inside of Mae's finger.

"Oh, poor girl," Lissy laughed and dabbed her finger into the blood. Then she smeared it into a little rough "L."

Mae started to take her hand away, but Lissy pulled it to her mouth and gave the palm a kiss. The dome light made Lissy's skin look a little yellow and bruised under, but her dark eyes were squinted and sparkling.

Without saying anything, Lissy came across the bench seat of the truck and put her smiling mouth on Mae's. At first Mae was too surprised, didn't do anything, but then the warm feel of lips and the sweet smell of

Lissy's skin let her relax. With her eyes shut, it was just lips on lips and she could let that kiss go on and on, but when she felt Lissy's hand, cool fingers and long nails, under her shirt, touching her bare stomach, Mae's eyes opened and she turned her head away.

"What's wrong?" Lissy asked. She was so close that Mae could smell the beer on her breath, feel the warmth on her cheek.

"Come on, Lissy."

"What?" Lissy moved closer still and tried to find Mae's mouth again. "It's okay."

"It's not. I'm not—"

"It won't mean anything, Mae." She kissed her again, just her lower lip, and moved her hand up the inside of Mae's leg. "You won't have to do anything." She talked as she kissed and Mae could feel Lissy's words on her mouth. Mae moved her hands to stop Lissy, but Lissy's hands were stronger and went farther, past Mae's fingers. She gave up and let herself go a little limp, stopped trying to fight.

Lissy stopped kissing her then and looked into Mae's eyes, before she turned away and pushed herself back across the seat. "Fuck it," she said, turning the keys in the ignition. "It was stupid."

"You're mad. Don't be mad."

"I'm not mad, Mae. I'm just drunk. Let's go home."

"You are mad, you are. Please."

"Damn it, Mae!" Lissy turned on her then, pushed her pleading hands away. "Stop."

"I love you, Lissy. You're my best friend. I don't want anything to be ruined." Mae watched as Lissy took two deep breaths.

"I love you too, Mae."

With each minute that Lissy didn't show up, Mae became more and more sure that there was something wrong with her that wouldn't let anyone really love her, only made them want to hurt her. Lou had been the best so far; maybe he'd be the best she could ever find; maybe she should take her bag back inside, push it into the closet and try to settle in.

She heard the truck before she saw it, bumping down the dirt road too fast, rattling into and out of potholes.

"What took you so long?" Mae asked as Lissy swung out of the truck and started over to the porch. Together they lifted Mae's bag and hefted it into the back of the truck. Lissy was wearing her tall leather boots and a denim miniskirt; her black hair was long and loose down her back. "Did you have a date?" Mae asked. She knew that Lissy had been seeing some real-estate guy named Brent pretty regular, that he'd been staying over most nights.

"Nah. Nobody special. You ready? Anything in there that you want to trash?" Lissy motioned to the house, which now looked even sadder and lonelier to Mae since it wasn't hers anymore. Mae shook her head and stepped up into the truck. It was only after Lissy had got into the other side and started the engine that Mae felt the tears start to come. She tried not to cry, to swallow them back; she didn't want to be this girl, but she was.

Mae started to sob, loud and gulping in that ugly, childish way.

Lissy cranked the radio and threw the truck into drive. She punched the gas so that the tires spun, shooting gravel against the house, onto the porch, and into the recliner.

"I really thought it would work this time," Mae said, watching the house get smaller in the mirror.

"I know you did, Mae," Lissy said, reaching across the seat and patting her hand. "But don't cry. You'll move back in, okay?"

Mae sniffled and watched the house disappear.

"And we'll get your job back at The Egg, no problem. It'll be just like old times. You'll forget all about Lou."

Mae wiped her face with her sleeve and reached to turn up the radio. "Who's Lou?"

Wanting Baby

———

*L*eigh pulled her car over into the grass, parking behind JR's battered GMC. A rebel flag stretched across the back cab window and silhouettes of two naked women with bent knees and erect nipples guarded either side of the tailgate. Gray's silver SUV was there, too; everybody already here, waiting for her.

Two weeks ago Maida called to confirm that Leigh was coming for Thanksgiving. Just hearing her voice had made Leigh feel a little safer, a little less out in the world alone, but now, as she sat there in the driveway, staring at the house after driving these three hours to West Virginia, she wasn't so sure this was a good idea.

Leigh's stomach rumbled a little and she felt a tiny punch from within. Baby knew they'd arrived and was telling her to move her ass.

Her foot sunk when she stepped out. The yard was a muddy mess that would freeze in the night, creating a frosted top that would make boot heels skid. The first time Trist brought her to the farm, she'd slipped on that, but Trist had been there to catch her.

By the time Leigh'd reached the porch, Maida was there, waiting for her. "Hey, Maida." Leigh put on a smile and waved. She smelled the aroma of turkey juices and brown sugar and burnt marshmallow from the candied yams that always ran over and sizzled on the bottom of the stove.

Maida wrapped Leigh in a quick hug and patted her on the back. "Good to see you," she said. "Just look. You're as big as a house. Won't be long now."

"Thank God," Leigh said and tried not to notice when Maida glanced over her shoulder toward the car, as if expecting someone else coming.

"I'm so glad you came," Maida said. "This is where you belong. You and that baby. Now come in here before you freeze." Maida turned and hustled back inside. Leigh took one final deep breath and pushed into the house, leaving the screen door *thrap* shut behind her.

Voices were coming from the living room, loud and comfortable, laughing and talking. Leigh could shut her eyes and picture the scene, she'd seen it enough times. It was like a concert; each member had their unique sound, their voice an instrument that played a certain way.

"Bullshit!" Gray's voice boomed out of the room, louder than all the others, the deep bass drum.

"Now, you can say 'bullshit' if you want to, but I'm telling you the way it is." JR, a little higher, a whinny. Leigh knew the story. It was the same story every year—the one about JR's miraculous shot that had felled some huge deer from behind a tree. Every year JR told that story and every year Gray refused to believe it. Trist had never believed it either, but never said so because he didn't want a confrontation. Gray and JR could tease and needle each other, but Trist and JR would fight. Leigh saw it happen once at Fourth of July when JR was drunk and red from sunburn. She hadn't heard what, but JR said something and Trist punched him. They were wrestling on the ground when Gray broke them up. She'd asked him about it later, but Trist just shrugged and said, "It's just the way it is with us. It don't mean nothing."

Leigh slipped off her muddy boots by the front door then slid into the room, not wanting to draw attention to herself and stop their good time. Jayce, Trist's younger sister; Gwen, JR's wife; and Lil, Gray's wife, were on one end of the room, talking and fussing over Gwen's three-year-old, Marlyn. Gray and JR were standing near the fire, smoking and dropping their ashes into the flames. Gray's and Lil's kids must have been outside or in another room. Baby would be part of that group, "the grandkids." Leigh wondered what her title was now. The wife of the dead son? The girl who used to be the son's wife?

Jayce saw her first. They locked eyes and Jayce's face quivered for a second then broke into a wide grin. "Leigh!"

Jayce pulled Leigh close and Leigh felt her round belly press into Jayce's flat one. Jayce had graduated high school in May but took a semester off before starting college. She was going after Christmas, leaving Maida and the house alone together.

"Why in the world didn't you say anything?" Everyone was quiet now, staring at Leigh.

"I just didn't want to interrupt," Leigh said.

"She always was a lurker," Gray said and pulled Leigh into a hug. He was Leigh's favorite, big and open in a way Trist never was. Gray and Trist had been close, the best of friends since they were boys, but they were different. He had cried the hardest at Trist's graveside and Lil had held him up; it looked like a mountain leaning on a speed bump.

Leigh made the rounds and hugged everyone, including thin-lipped, smart-assed Gwen. Trist had called her "the bleached chicken." With her skinny legs, long neck, and unnaturally blond hair pulled up in a topknot, Gwen looked like she might start clucking and scratching the ground at any moment. But there was something different, a little fullness of her face, a thickening around her middle.

"Only about three and a half months," Gwen said, noticing Leigh's eyes on her middle.

"I didn't know," Leigh said. "Congratulations."

"Oh, thanks. Have to keep that family line going, you know." Leigh could smell Gwen's perfume, something heavy that was probably dark brown and called "Sexy Mama" or "Hot Seduction." It made Leigh feel like the inside of her nose was swelling, but Gwen wouldn't move away. "We were just so surprised when Maida said you were coming! We figured you'd be spending the holiday with your family this year." Gwen just blinked her overly mascaraed eyes and cocked her head a little. She knew, they all knew, Leigh had no family.

"Well, Maida asked and you know how hard it is to say no to her," Leigh shifted her weight and disengaged herself from Gwen's arms.

"Well, I knew Leigh would come," Jayce said and put her arm around Leigh's waist. "Because she loves us." She smiled and Leigh did too; she did love them, as well as she knew how.

Maida was standing at the stove stirring a pot of gravy, her whole arm working from shoulder to wrist. Trist said that when he thought of home and Maida, this was how he saw her, in the kitchen, stirring or peeling. If some other boy had said this, Leigh would have thought it sexist, but Trist didn't mean it that way, didn't think a woman's place was in the kitchen. And after meeting Maida, she'd never have mistaken her for being a slave to her family. Dinner, every dinner, was just so important to the family. It meant being together and sharing food and the day, and Maida was the facilitator of all that. Those were the warm feelings Trist had wanted to bring with him and conjure when he was away from home, eating dorm food or takeout.

Leigh rarely thought about her own mother, and when she did, she saw a tall woman with dark hair down her back and black, smudgy circles under her eyes from melted makeup. She worked a lot at some low-paying office temp job and went out at night, leaving Leigh at first with babysitters and then alone. She died when Leigh was twelve, and Leigh cried because she felt something was gone, some chance at a mother and a family, but her actual mother being gone barely felt any different at all. Then, all through high school, she was the girl whose mom had died or the girl who lived with her grandparents. She was so happy to go to college and be someone new that she hardly thought about home at all. She got an apartment and a part-time job. She only went home twice: once her freshman year for her grandmother's funeral and again the next year for her grandfather's. What a pair she and Trist made: the boy with so much family he could take them with him anywhere and the girl with no family at all.

She thought maybe that's what happened to all families when a parent died—everyone just drifted their own ways until finally there was nothing left to connect them, but after she met Trist, she knew this wasn't so. His father had died of a heart attack when Trist was fourteen and instead of falling apart, the family came together, took care of one another, held each other up.

"Oh! Well, Leigh," Maida said, surprised when she turned and saw Leigh in the doorway. "I didn't see you there."

"Sorry, Maida. Do you need any help?"

"Ah, no, I've got it under control." Maida leaned against the counter, crossed her arms and ankles. "How is work, Leigh?"

"Fine. It's fine." Except that she was on a yearlong sabbatical from teaching, not to do research or to write, but so that she wouldn't have to do either. "I don't know how I'll go back once Baby comes."

"Well, who says you have to?" Maida smiled to let Leigh know she knew how silly that was. "I do wish you lived closer though. When Jayce leaves for school, it's sure gonna be quiet around here."

"I understand quiet," Leigh said.

"Any trouble with the house?"

"No, the buyers seemed nice enough. Most of our things are in storage, but the apartment is fine."

"Well you know you and the baby are always welcome here, Leigh." She turned again to stir the gravy. For just a moment, Leigh wanted to reach out to Maida, to touch her shoulder and say, "You and me, we're alike. We both lost husbands; we both loved Trist. We're just the same."

In the hallway was a parade of senior pictures. Young Gray, black haired and serious; Trist with such a big smile and wispy blond hair; JR wearing tight jeans, tucked into unlaced work boots, trying to look tough and brooding. Trist looked to all the world like a free spirit, open and warm, and he was that in his own way, but it wasn't easy to see. He was hard, was happy alone with his hands in the dirt, and she'd nearly given up on him a few times, would have too if not for that glimmer of something else, something deeper. It was almost like he had some secret, some special thing, and she was the only one who could search it out. She'd spent years trying, but never got to the core.

Leigh stopped and rubbed her fingers over the glass of Trist's picture, leaving a greasy fingerprint across his shiny face. Three years after he was a junior studying environmental science and she was in the last semester of her English degree. The first time she saw him, he was sitting on the grass outside the English department, not studying, but just sitting there alone, looking completely content. Leigh never would have done that. She would have felt too uncomfortable, too much like everyone was watching and wondering what she was doing, sitting there all alone. Didn't she have any friends?

Always, Trist was content just to be by himself because he didn't have to be. He always knew that, no matter what, there was a good group of people thinking of him, waiting for him to come home. He gave that to Leigh, at least a little. Coming to the farm for Thanksgiving was an attempt to hold on, to make it last, but Leigh felt that life slipping, faster and faster.

Back in the front room, Lil, Gwen, and Jayce were playing with Marlyn. She was in the middle of the room, singing "The Wheels on the Bus," leading everyone through the motions. Gwen was mouthing the words along with her, and when everyone clapped, Gwen nearly took a bow.

"Where are the guys?" Leigh asked.

"I think they're all out hunting," Lil said. "Gray's determined our oldest is going to get his first buck this year, but I don't know."

"I hate it," Jayce said. "It's so barbaric. Trist—" She stopped herself and looked quickly at Leigh.

"It's okay, Jayce. You can talk about him," Leigh said.

"I was just going to say that Trist would never hunt. Daddy wanted him to and he'd go out with all the boys, but never got anything. Then, one time, Daddy found him out there, sitting up in a tree, studying the leaves."

"That sounds like Trist," Lil said. It did sound like Trist, and Leigh's face grew hot with the realization that all these women, even Gwen, had known Trist longer than she had.

"So, when is the baby due again, Leigh?" Gwen asked.

"Oh, December 10. Pretty soon."

"Are you nervous?" Jayce asked. "I'd be scared shitless."

"Not so much about the birth," Leigh said. "More about after. I've never really been around kids."

"Oh, it will all come naturally," Lil said and pulled Marlyn up into her lap.

"That's what they say." But I don't believe a damn word of it, Leigh thought. She looked at Marlyn, a cute child in a red velvet holiday dress with lace on the collar, and tried to manage some maternal urge to protect her or love her, cuddle her, play with her, but she couldn't. Trist was the gardener. He planted seeds and nurtured them until they bloomed strong and beautiful. Leigh killed cactuses.

I am in such trouble, Leigh thought, not for the first time.

"I'm surprised the doctor even wanted you traveling, this close to your due date," Gwen said, taking Marlyn from Lil and giving her a quick kiss on the cheek. A peck. Leigh thought again about the bleached chicken. Trist would laugh his ass off at Gwen's new orange from-the-bottle tan. She was turning more into poultry every year.

"Well, I didn't really ask," Leigh said. Jayce laughed like she'd made a joke, but she hadn't.

"Been thinking about names?" Gwen asked.

"Well, right now I'm just going with Baby."

"You know, Tristan *is* a family name," Gwen said.

"Gwen—" In Lil's voice was a warning and Leigh could tell this wasn't the first time Gwen had brought up this subject.

"Usually it's the second son, you know. That's why Trist was given the name instead of Gray, but since—" Lil cleared her throat. Gwen continued to chew her gum and moved her head around a little, as if she was looking for a bug to peck. *B-bock.*

"Gwen, shut up," Jayce said. She was even starting to stand up, as if she'd strike Gwen if she said another word. Gwen continued to pop and chomp her gum like a teenager.

Leigh felt sick to her stomach; she didn't know if she wanted to name the baby Tristan. The baby would have enough pressure, being the last bit of Trist left; he or she shouldn't have to be saddled with his name too. But damn Gwen.

"What?" Gwen asked.

"Gwen, you're such a bitch," Jayce said.

"What?!" Gwen set Marlyn down and stood glaring with her hands—long, pointy red nails like daggers—claws—on her hips.

"Don't pay any attention to Gwen. She's just an idiot," Jayce said, still glaring at her sister-in-law. "What's wrong with you, Gwen?"

"What are you making such a fuss about, Jayce? That name's important to your family and you know well as I do that she ain't going to come around without Trist. I just think that the family name should stay *in the family*. No offense, Leigh." Gwen's eyes were bulging, liquid orbs under those thick, spidery eyelashes. Leigh felt her stomach roll and knew she'd be sick if she didn't get out.

I'm not in the family, she thought. Gwen's right.

Leigh wished she could move faster, but the chair was low and she couldn't just stand straight up. Finally, she had to roll out of the chair and onto her knee, then pull herself up by the chair's arms while the other women watched. "I think I'm going to go lay down for a couple of minutes. It was a long drive."

She went to Trist's room, the place he'd spent his first eighteen years and where they had spent their nights together when they visited the farm. The bed was so tiny that even with Leigh's back against the wall and Trist's elbow digging into her side, his left leg still dangled off the edge. It was uncomfortable, but she loved lying there, picturing him at different stages in his life—playing cars on the rug, building model planes, sitting at his desk studying geometry. She teased him about all the girls he'd fantasized about between those sheets. "So how does it feel having a real live woman in your bed?" She traced the lines on his chest and stomach with her finger.

"A little creepy," he said, staring up at the ceiling where a glow-in-the-dark solar system still glowed.

Leigh was glad the rodeo sheets were still there. They were blue and dotted with lassoing cowboys. Maida hadn't changed a thing about the room—not thrown out an old comic book or bought a new pillow for the bed. She'd always made it look like it was waiting for Trist, so he would feel welcome when he came home for a visit.

Leigh buried her face in the scratchy blue linens. She breathed deeply and wanted so badly to smell Trist there that she imagined she did for a moment. She pushed her back against the wall and shut her eyes. She waited, hoping to feel an indention in the mattress beside her, to feel a body press up against her and fit together in the awkward but perfect way of jagged puzzle pieces.

If she could just stay here, sleep in this bed every night, smell his smells, touch his things, maybe she could still fit.

She shut her eyes and tried to dream of Trist. She once heard you dream about whatever is in your head when you drift off. She'd been having a recurring dream lately of Baby, a pink little mass floating around and smiling. She never saw herself in the dream, but was there, watching Baby as if it all were a show on TV. Baby remained just out of her reach, teasing and tumbling, tempting her to chase. Leigh could see her own hands, reaching and grasping, coming up empty.

But now she couldn't sleep and after trying every trick she knew—counting sheep, crossing her eyes—she finally gave up and counted the ceiling tiles.

"Are you decent?" She heard Gray's voice, muffled through the thick door. "Leigh, are you decent?" She woke herself enough to realize the voice wasn't Baby's but Gray's, just outside the bedroom door.

"You can come in," she mumbled. She tried to sit but felt too much like a beach ball and gave up.

"Were you asleep? Mom sent me up. Dinner's about ready." Gray came in and stood above her, looking down and trying not to laugh.

"What's so funny?"

"Nothing. Just seeing you, lying there all big and miserable in that little bed. We all had those; they're like half beds or something. Need some help up?"

"I think I'll just stay here."

"Ah, shit, Leigh. Jayce told me what Gwen said. You know she's an idiot. Don't let her bother you."

"But she's right, isn't she? Aren't you all thinking it?"

"Thinking what? That she's an idiot? Hell yes."

"Don't make jokes, Gray," Leigh's arm fell across her face so that she wouldn't have to look at him.

"It's a hard thing, Leigh. Especially for Mom."

Leigh lifted her arm just enough to see him through one eye as he lowered himself into the tiny desk chair.

"She's been having a hard time lately. She doesn't let on, but after Trist . . . and now with Jayce leaving too. . . . It's the first time in her life she's going to be alone."

Where was all this going? Leigh got a little flutter in her chest and the unbelievable thought that maybe he really was going to ask her to move here, to live in this big, empty house with Maida. It seemed crazy, but maybe it wasn't. Maybe what Maida had said when they were in the kitchen hadn't been a joke after all.

"Lil and I aren't far, but it's not the same, you know?" Gray said and Leigh felt Baby give a little internal jab. She could see herself walking and touching and breathing where Trist had walked and touched and breathed for so long. She could see herself tucking Baby between those rodeo sheets. She could have a little garden.

"I think she's really scared," Gray said. Leigh looked over at him just as he was wiping his eyes. She reached out and touched his hand.

"I know it's not fair to ask you, Leigh. I know what you've been through—"

"It's okay," Leigh said. "Go ahead."

"It's just, if you could talk to Mom, let her know that you'll still come around after the baby's born. Just give her some security that she can still be a part of his or her life. I know it'd make her feel better. It'd be one less thing to worry about."

"Oh." Leigh felt that sinking feeling of disappointment but tried not to let it show. She suddenly knew what it felt like to be one of those women who were wanted only for their looks or their money. She was wanted just for her baby.

"You have to understand, Leigh. It's the last part of Trist. To think of losing that—"

"I understand." She tried to keep the coldness out of her voice. It wasn't Gray's fault, and if anyone could understand wanting to hold on to a piece of Trist, it was her. "I really do. I want Baby to be part of your family. I wouldn't have it any other way."

After Gray left, Leigh lay there for a few moments, pulled the sheets up to her face, tried to imagine what it was like to grow up here. Baby prodded her gently from within, maybe to tell her she wouldn't be alone, maybe to tell her to get up. The two weren't really that different.

Every holiday meal was a free-for-all with arms and hands and fingers everywhere. At first Leigh had been intimidated. She'd hung back, watching the family fight for food before finding their seats, but Trist pulled her in, shoved a plate in her hands. He had looked so happy, so at home that Leigh laughed and grabbed the sweet-potato spoon out of Gray's hand. "Thatta girl!" Trist had said and Gray had smacked her shoulder.

When Leigh came downstairs, everyone was already in the kitchen. They were quiet when they first saw Leigh, until Maida smiled and said, "Now you all make room for Leigh. A pregnant woman shouldn't have to fight for her food."

"No, that's all right," Leigh said. She'd been hanging back, not because she didn't want to join the fray, but because she was enjoying the normalcy of it all and trying to make it into a memory.

"Damn right," JR said and winked at Leigh.

When everyone was done and seated, Maida asked Gray to say grace.

"Dear Lord," Gray said, his voice scratchy and uncertain. "Thank you for this meal Mom has put before us and for bringing us all together on this day of Thanksgiving. We all have much to be thankful for, even though this has been a difficult year. Sometimes you work in mysterious ways and we don't understand the things you do, Lord, but we thank you for helping us through the hard times and keeping us together as a family. Thank you, Lord, for bringing us together today and for the babies who will soon be joining our family. Please, Lord, watch over our father and our dear brother Trist." Leigh felt that familiar sting at her heart to remind her that she was alive, but wounded. She tried to summon up the warmth that spread up from her feet, a feeling she'd got that first Thanksgiving, when Trist had grabbed her hand under the table and squeezed, but she didn't feel anything.

Baby kicked a little and she put her hand in the spot, just the fabric of her clothes and the thin veil of skin between her hand and Baby's tiny foot. Baby would come here and be part of this family. On long weekends and summer vacations, Baby would sleep in the tiny half bed and look at the glowing solar system overhead. And for a while she could come too, pretend, hold on. Baby was the band that held her to Trist's family, but the band would get thinner and thinner as Baby grew, until finally there would be just a thread, still there but nearly invisible.

"Leigh?" Jayce said and touched Leigh's arm.

"I'm okay," Leigh said, then picked up her fork and began to eat.

Lettuce

We see the sky getting dark and Matt goes out to cover the lettuce. He wants the vegetables safe and unbruised, has tarps and buckets collected in the outbuilding for just such an occasion. I've learned not to ask if he wants help. When I used to offer, he thought I figured he couldn't do it himself. But it wasn't like that.

Or maybe it was. It doesn't matter anymore.

The clouds roll in and I watch him cover his lettuce from the kitchen window, remembering the time I was ten and visiting my aunt in Illinois. We had a storm, what the news people said was a derecho, like a wall of hell. A horizontal tornado, some said, but it rolled more like a hurricane. It lasted a long time, and I was crying before it was over.

When we looked at the sky, the layers of dark heavy clouds, I was sure it was the end of the world. But it finally cleared, and people picked up, cleaned up, moved on.

The rain starts falling fast and hard. I see Matt stoop, but he doesn't want to sacrifice the tender lettuce. He puts the tarp over some, weighs it down with big rocks. He places buckets over the tomato and pepper plants. Then the hail comes, pellets hitting the roof of the porch, tinny and loud. Matt tries to cover himself by holding his nonarm over his head, but he doesn't quit, because now his work is even more important. Some wives would run out, grab an umbrella or a pot or something. I stand and watch, wondering how long it will take him to give in.

Before the storm came, I'd been grating carrots for a salad. Matt is a vegetarian now. This has irritated me from the beginning, not because I care about the food, but because it seems so predictable, like something that would happen in a movie. That's what this all feels like sometimes—not our real life, but some melodramatic, made-for-TV movie. Boy goes off to war, sees unspeakable, loses left arm in an IED explosion, can't stomach the blood and flesh of meat anymore. It's not that I don't have any compassion either. I was nothing but compassion, a giant pudding ball of compassion, until I couldn't be anymore.

When I was grating carrots, I heard a car coming up the drive. Really, it wasn't in our drive, just going slow up the bumpy dirt road, but as I jumped to look, I slipped. The carrot nub flipped out of my hand, and my knuckles went down hard and fast across those sharp teeth. It took a minute to sink in, the way it does when you hurt yourself in some stupid way and can't look down for fear of what you'll see. Pictures flashed in my head of shredded skin, white knucklebone shining through blood and gore. I grabbed a dishtowel and pressed it to my knuckles, but when I looked down I saw a few tiny drops of blood in the salad bowl. The red was bold and hot against the orange of the carrots, and I knew that I should throw it all out. But the big wooden bowl was full of tomatoes, lettuce, cucumbers, and peppers. Throwing it out would be wasteful, and there wasn't time to run to town for more vegetables.

This was how I told it to myself. And when I came back downstairs after washing my hand and bandaging my knuckles, I mixed the carrot shreds up good so the bloody spots were gone. That's what I did and I'm not sorry.

"Son of a bitch came on fast," Matt says when he bangs in, soaking wet and dripping all over the kitchen floor. "I think I got it in time. Hope I did."

"I'm sure you did," I say, but I don't have much in my voice to convince him. He doesn't notice, so I don't try too hard.

"I don't remember the weatherman saying it was going to rain today, do you? Is it still hailing? You know what they say about hail." Matt looks out the window, though we can hear the ice bouncing off the porch roof. They say hail is sometimes a sign a tornado is coming, but I don't know what Matt means anymore. He could mean anything.

"You're dripping," I say. "You shouldn't track that mud upstairs. Just strip your clothes here, then go put on something dry." His face goes a little funny because he doesn't like the idea. "Come on, Matt. It's a mess."

"Fine," he says. I cross my arms as he pushes off his boots, then, one-handed, undoes his buckle, button, and zipper; he sloughs his wet jeans off like a snake losing his skin. His boxers are wet through, but I decide not to push it. I wonder if he'll leave the nonarm on as he tries to get his wet T-shirt off, or if he'll release this contraption I hate. I see he's also wondering which would be best.

He doesn't like for anyone to see his scars, not even me, and it's not because of vanity. Matt is a good-looking man, always has been, but doesn't try too hard. No hair gel or fancy clothes. He still wears the same brand of drugstore cologne his mother bought him when he started shaving, even through the army, even still. I think he's afraid the scars and stump and machine-like parts of the nonarm make him look weaker.

He already feels weak, even after all the months in physical therapy, even though his good arm is stronger than most two put together. Some men get to hide their damage, but Matt has to wear his—artificial flesh toned and creepy veiny—every day.

It took a while, but now he can dress and undress himself, take care of his bathroom things. He can do garden work and some of the farm work for his daddy, like drive the tractor. "Use the arm," the therapists told him. "It's not like the old prosthetics. These new pieces are incredible."

At first, they wanted to give him a hi-tech, robot-like one that could grasp cups. It was an experimental model and they tried to tell me how it worked—something about nerves being rerouted, muscles in the chest learning to twitch in a way that would make the fingers move. I didn't understand. When they showed me, I couldn't stop staring at the icy silver of it.

"Matt would be able to hold your hand," one therapist said. She was a young girl with bright eyes, a long, curled ponytail, intricately applied makeup. She wasn't much younger than us, but she seemed like a kid. To her, the idea of Matt being able to hold my hand again probably sounded sweet, romantic.

I touched the robot hand and tried to imagine the cool fingers beginning to tighten. I thought I felt a twitch and jerked away.

"What good is this doing?" Matt asked the girl. "I'll never be able to feel her hand. Why would I ever do this in real life?"

My cheeks went red then, imagining real life and what he might do with his bionic arm. Images flashed in my head of our bedroom, Matt saying, "Look how my chest muscles make my fingers close. Look how I can move them on you." I felt a sick quake in my stomach and had to get up. I was outside the door quick, and slid down the wall.

The pretty girl couldn't understand. She met men like Matt and wives like me every day, but then she went home to her boyfriend who still has everything he's supposed to have. Some farm boy who still has his twinkle, who holds her and undresses her and touches her with two warm hands.

"That's the last time she's in here," I heard Matt say to the girl.

Matt has a different sort of arm now. This one fastens around his body with thick straps and is still incredible, but not quite as incredible as the robotic one. He thought that one scared me, and that I was embarrassed. He told the therapist it just didn't feel right, that maybe he wasn't strong enough for that yet. So instead he has one that looks more like "the real thing" from the elbow down. The hand is always slightly bent, ready for gripping. The doctors say that the technology is improving all the time, especially now with such demand. Matt tells me he's on a list to get a better arm permanently. I read about it on the internet—the "Luke" they call it, after Luke Skywalker's bionic arm in the Star Wars movies.

Matt struggles, trying to get the wet T-shirt up and over his nonarm. Normally he could do it, but the shirt is wet and stuck to his skin. "Okay, Jenny," he says finally. "Help me."

I peel gently from the bottom, first over his good arm so he can help, then over the nonarm, then over his head. I'm close enough that I can see the little welts on his shoulders and forehead where the hail hit him. That's when I remember to listen, and hear that it's stopped.

"Just rain now," I say, and realize I'm still holding the shirt above his head and that our chests are touching. On my tiptoes I can just reach his lips because he is tall and I am not. I'm surprised that I kiss him because I didn't think I would. My hand is in his hair, long now, grown out, so that I can grab it, wrap my hand up in it like he used to in mine.

"Jen," he says around my lips, but I keep my hand in his hair, and kiss him so hard that I taste blood in my mouth, his or mine I don't know. If he would take off the arm, I would lick his scars. When he's awake, he won't let me touch them, doesn't want me to look, but sometimes when he's asleep, I kneel on the floor beside the bed and run my finger around each purple crevice, each indention. I cup the missing piece. The pills make him sleep deep and I'm glad, because if he woke to find me there, he would howl. He'd push me and my kisses away like he does every time.

I pull his hair, force his head back and kiss his throat.

"What's gotten into you?" he says. He's trying to move away, trying to laugh me off, but I don't want to let him go. How would the movie go? If we were living out this drama on the screen, would he push me away now, again, or would this be the climax where Matt finally lets me unstrap his nonarm and then lies down on the cold kitchen tiles? Would he cry? Would the hail start again, or the lightning and thunder, rolling over us?

I used to love those nights when the air got thick with electricity. The thunder rolled around the house in waves, the lightning showing Matt to me in flashes as it lit up the bedroom. When it was over, there was just the slow, soft rain. We'd lie close together. I knew everything then.

With his good hand, Matt pats my shoulder. "Isn't it about time for dinner?" he asks. "I'll go get some dry clothes on. Okay?" He's using his hand to disentangle mine from his hair. He doesn't want to hurt me. He just wants to go.

I watch him gather his wet clothes from the floor. I think I should get the mop and take care of the puddles, but I don't. Instead, I get the vegetarian lasagna from the oven. I get the salad from the refrigerator.

The storm has somehow circled us and, when we sit to eat, the rain is loud again. When the thunder comes, I can feel it in my whole body as the house shudders.

"Here it comes again," Matt says. He's wearing a blue T-shirt from high school, with the school mascot—a wildcat—on the front. His hair is in his eyes. He looks so young, so much younger than I feel. How unfair that he can look like that and I have to feel like this. His nonarm is resting on the table. He's waiting for me to serve him.

"This looks good," he says as I cut the lasagna and scoop it onto his plate. I'm not a good cook, especially when it comes to dishes where delicate vegetables are expected to pull together and make something hearty.

"Have some salad." I use the plastic tongs to fill our bowls to the top. I spear some with my fork but don't put it to my mouth until Matt takes a mouthful, mostly lettuce, streaked with shreds of orange. He chews and when he sees me watching, he smiles.

"At least I can make salad," I say. I take my bite, already knowing that after he goes to sleep tonight, I'll sneak out and drive the forty-five minutes to Morgantown to get a greasy fast food cheeseburger. Maybe two.

My Brothers and Me

———

JD, my brother, built a fire and was burning anything. First, he'd started with branches, underbrush that he'd cleared the week before, but then other things. Boxes. Junk mail and newspapers. Someone had mentioned an old wooden table they'd had in storage for a while. Robby, another brother, threw in some old wiring and the flames turned blue, purple, green.

This was four days after our brother Jeff had killed his wife by shooting her in the trailer that sat just two or three hundred yards from where we were. My brothers all lived close together, close to my parents, all on the same few acres of property that had been in my family for nearly one hundred years. Jeff was the youngest boy, only I was after him. JD was the oldest; Robby right in the middle.

JD had heard the gunshot and got there first. He'd heard Jeff and Christine fighting, but hadn't thought much about it. They were always fighting, yelling, throwing things. Once, Christine had gotten so mad that she'd thrown a butcher knife at Jeff, but it had only nicked his shoulder. Once, Jeff had gotten so mad that he'd thrown a lamp at Christine, but it had missed and instead broke the large picture window that faced the road. For nearly a month after that, anyone driving past saw the boarded-up window, later evidence.

When JD heard the shot, he went to Jeff's trailer. He started out slow enough, but when he got closer, he said, he heard a different kind of screaming, a keening that he hadn't heard anything like before, so he picked up his pace. Christine was lying on the living-room floor. There's no way to tell it that doesn't sound like a cliché. Like a thousand stories you've heard on TV before and think nothing about until it's your brother and his wife, who'd also been your friend since high school. That's when you say things like "a pool of blood" and "dead" and they mean something.

Jeff had thought he'd miss. He always missed. But he hadn't, or he had missed what he'd been aiming for, maybe, and instead hit Christine in the chest.

JD said that Jeff was wailing, just wailing, and running his hands over Christine without touching her, just over and over. "Jesus Christ," JD said. "Jesus, Jeff. Jesus Christ."

I do not live where my brothers live. I moved away, but not far, only forty miles or so to be closer to the university where I work as an administrative assistant. I help students register for their classes and apply for financial aid. I do paperwork and make phone calls and sit at the front desk. I dress nice and tame my curly wild hair as much as I can so that I can be the professional face of the office. I was married, so my last name is not the same as my brothers'. When my brother shot his wife, and the story came out in all the local newspapers, I did not have to say a thing. I sat at my desk, and pretended that I was not this person, for as long as I could, until JD called to ask if I'd come to the courthouse for the preliminary trial where a judge would decide whether Jeff could get bonded out. I had to ask for time off and tell why. My last name became Dixon again for the first time since I'd married Jess Brantly ten years before.

I was sitting near the fire, in an old lawn chair, seat sunk so low that my butt nearly touched the ground. No one was really talking;

we'd all just found our way here. JD's wife Tanya had been by me for a while, but then went to get her kids some sticks for hot dogs. Someone might have said to them that this wasn't that kind of fire, but when kids see a fire outdoors, they want to roast a wiener and some marshmallows. And what was the harm, really?

JD and Robby were drinking, then throwing their beer cans or bottles into the fire where they mostly just sat, the cans turning black and the paper peeling from the bottles. I was holding a bottle, too, but hadn't really been drinking from it. Just turning it around in my hands and feeling it get warm.

It was early May, but cool. The weather had been off this year—barely any snow all winter, temperatures in the eighties in March, then a snowstorm in April. Now, May, feeling almost normal with warmish days and coolish nights, but I still felt strange, like my body had never adjusted to the lack of an extreme winter. Maybe that's what had been happening to everyone, going crazy like on a full moon because of the seasons. In a county where you could usually count the number of murders from the last five years on one hand, there'd been three in the last month. First that lady whose father-in-law shot her in the Walmart parking lot over a custody fight. Then that murder/suicide in Independence. Then. Then.

JD had a theory about chain reactions; Robby thought maybe it was the crap economy that had everybody on edge. I didn't think. I tried, but my brain just spun. I was restless and unfocused but couldn't do anything. I'd try to work, or have a conversation, but then I'd remember, my brother in a jail cell. My brother wearing that orange jumpsuit. My brother today in the courtroom with his hands and ankles shackled. I wanted to tell them how unnecessary that was. He was a danger to no one but himself.

I hadn't gone home after court but came right here in my dressy work clothes. Tanya'd found me a pair of stretchy workout shorts—the only thing of hers that I could fit into since she was a tiny, tiny woman—and a pair of flip-flops so I wouldn't have to walk around outside in my poky high-heeled boots. I was also wearing an old sweatshirt that I'd found in my parents' house. It was mine from years before, from high school. The insignia of the black knight on the front had started to wear and peel. It was huge on me now—had been huge on me then, but that was the way I'd liked it, and tonight it felt right to cuddle up inside something from the past.

"Mari." Robby came up behind me and squeezed my shoulders. He was getting drunk. I could tell because he was wanting to hug and was slurring his words. He took the bottle of warm beer from my hands and replaced it with a cold one from the cooler. "Drink," he said, then walked away.

My cell phone in the front pouch pocket of my sweatshirt began to vibrate. I took it out and saw that it was Marcus, again. He'd been calling all day, sometimes leaving voice mail, and sometimes just hanging up when I didn't answer. Marcus was the man I was seeing—which sounded more grown up than saying that he was my boyfriend. I still had my own apartment, but stayed with him most of the time, since he had a nice house in the nice part of town walking distance from campus where a lot of the faculty lived. He was a nice man, a sociology professor on the fast track to tenure. He wore pressed jeans, a button-up shirt, and a tie—a carefully developed uniform so that he looked both professional and approachable to his students.

"Hi," I said. I'd put him off long enough.

"Marianne, I've been trying to reach you all day," he said, and the relief in his voice instantly made me feel guilty.

"I know. I'm sorry. I've just been . . . I don't know. I'm with my family."

"Of course. Of course. I understand. I was just worried."

"I'm sorry," I said again, and then there was silence. That silence was why I hadn't wanted to answer the phone. We didn't really know what to say to each other. Emotionally, Marcus understood that I had to love my brother, that I would sit behind him in the courtroom and give what money I could to his defense; but intellectually, it didn't make sense for me to do it. My brother was a murderer, and no one was even trying to say otherwise. Marcus was ruled by his intellect, but we today we were ruled by our emotions—our love and fear and confusion. He didn't know what to say to that.

"Do you want me to come there?" he said, finally. I smiled a little. It was a nice effort, and he almost sounded as though he meant it. God, though, what a disaster that would be. Marcus was a good man, a great scholar, and he was always on. If he came here tonight, my family would ultimately and automatically become a sociological study.

"No, no. It's okay. I just need to be with my family right now. JD's built a fire, and we're just all sitting around."

"Of course, of course," he said again, and I imagined him making notes about the rituals of grieving.

"And you have lots of work to do. I'll probably just stay here tonight." I thought of crawling into the tiny bed in my parents' spare bedroom, the room that used to be mine, and wanted to sob. I felt it well up, painful in my throat, but swallowed it back down.

"Please call me if you need anything. Call even if you don't, okay?" Marcus sounded like he was nearly ready to cry, and that made me want to laugh. What did he have to cry about?

"I will," I said.

"And I'll see you tomorrow, right?"

"Sure, of course." Out of the corner of my eye, I saw Andrea and Matt, my teenage niece and nephew, making kissing faces in my direction. I managed a weak smile. Matt was sixteen. I saw that he had a beer sitting by his foot; JD had given it to him earlier and no one had protested. Marcus would have been sure to note that.

"I love you," Marcus said, a rare confession of feeling on his part. I glanced at Andrea and Matt.

"Okay, me too. See you tomorrow," I said and then quickly hung up before he could say anything else.

"Ooh, Aunt Mari. Is that your fancy boyfriend?" Andrea said.

"He's not so fancy. You guys are brats."

"Why ain't *he* here?" Matt said, at once asking a question and making a statement. The way Matt said *he* made it pretty clear how he felt, what he knew, and that he didn't really need an answer. I just shrugged.

"He has work," I said.

Jeff worked for Shaffer Trucking, had since he graduated high school. He drove a coal truck, usually just loads within a hundred miles or so, asphalt for the road crews, sometimes gravel or dirt. He made a living. His handle for the CB radio was Marshall Dixon because our last name sort of sounded like Dillon—Marshall Dillon from that old show *Gunsmoke*—and Jeff was sort of known for being a rule follower among the guys. He didn't like to take loads over the legal limit, though most all of them did, and he wouldn't lie on his time card. Now, I wished that he had. A little more money in his pocket. What difference would it have made after this?

"Who's coming?" Robby said. The property sat well off the road, at the end of a long dirt drive, and we could hear a car coming down long before we could see it. The first day or so my brothers had had some trouble with reporters, wanting pictures of Jeff's house, wanting interviews with my parents and JD since he'd found Christine. It hadn't taken much to get most of them to quit coming. Some of the local reporters knew us, from high school or just from being around, and they'd only come once, more out of professional duty than journalistic curiosity. The ones from Morgantown, the bigger town next door where I lived, were a little harder to convince, but JD can be big, intimidating, when he wants to be, and I guess they weren't going to take the chance that killers ran in our family. Still though, my brothers were jumpy at the sound of the tires crunching on the dirt and gravel.

"Matt," JD said to his son. "Go get my bat."

Matt started to get up, but Robby stopped him.

"He won't need it," he said. "That ain't no reporter."

"It's Jess," JD said as the big gray truck exited the tree line. Jess Brantley, my ex-husband.

I can't say I was surprised to see him there, and neither were my brothers. We'd all known Jess most of our lives, in one way or another. He and my brothers were good friends growing up, and then he was my husband, and then he wasn't, but they'd stayed friendly. I suppose some people would've been mad about that, like my brothers weren't being loyal through the divorce, but it felt right to me. He'd been theirs first, really, coming home with them on the school bus to ride dirt bikes or shoot BB guns. I was just an annoying little sister for years, until one night when Jess drove a different truck down that driveway to see me.

It was getting dark and in the fading light, I could just see Jess's figure get out of the truck and slam the door. I was looking through the fire, saw him like some specter, dark image from my past.

"Who's that?" My father had stepped out onto the porch of my parents' house, looking tired and yellow in the porch light. Old. I had never seen my parents look so old.

"It's just Jess, Daddy," JD shouted, and my father nodded before turning to go back inside, as though he'd been expecting him all along.

"Did somebody call Jess?" I asked Tanya, who was sitting on the ground beside me again.

She shrugged. "Not that I know of. Guess he just wanted to come by."

"Well, shit," I said, and pushed myself up out of the sinking lawn chair. As I walked towards Jess, I remembered how ridiculous I must look in my giant old sweatshirt and Tanya's tiny shorts. I tried to pat down my hair that had gone curly and huge in the humidity of the night.

JD was hugging Jess, hugging him for too long, and when they separated, JD wiped at his eyes. He slapped Jess on the back and said, "Thanks for coming. I'm glad you're here."

Jess and I locked eyes, and he watched my face as he hugged Tanya and Robby and Robby's girlfriend Dina. Some of the little kids ran up and grabbed him too. The older ones—Matt and Andrea—just waved from the fire.

"I'm going to go in and see your mom and daddy," he said to Robby. He wasn't going to come to me, I realized, maybe because he thought I didn't want him to, but I'd come over from the fire. I'd come halfway to him. That was always the problem. He couldn't learn to meet me halfway. I turned away, starting to go back to my seat, but then felt a hand on my elbow.

"Hey, Marianne," he said, still holding my sleeve. "You doing okay?"

"Hey, Jess," I said. His hair was shorter than the last time I'd seen him, but still black as coal, and his skin was tanned from working outside, which made his eyes look like two pieces of blue ice. He put his arms around me, awkward at first, and said "Maise" near my ear. That was my nickname when we were young; no one called me that anymore. When Jess said "Maise" it was like something unlocked inside me, like I hadn't been called my own name in years. I put my arms around him, slipping them beneath the thin jacket he was wearing and pressing my cheek to his T-shirt chest, smelling the woodsy cologne he'd worn since he was thirteen.

"Do you want me to go?" he said. "I will, if you want. I just felt like I needed to be here."

"Stay," I said.

"Uncle Jess," Robby's little girl Lily said. "Uncle Jess, you know I got a lamb?" I felt the rumble of Jess's soft laugh in his chest.

"Is that right?" he said and let me go. "I'll be darned."

"Want to see it? It's out by the barn."

"Maybe later, Lily girl." Jess brushed his hand across the top of her head. Lily looked up at him adoringly—all kids loved Jess, always had.

"Do you remember that year when you got that lamb, Maise? We'd sing that song to you, Marianne had a little lamb. It'd make her so mad she'd cry," he said to Lily and she laughed. I realized then how close I was still standing to Jess, that I still had my hands under his jacket, and backed away. "You even put a dog collar and dog leash on him, remember?"

"That was a long time ago," I said. "Too long ago to talk about."

"Yeah," Jess said, no longer smiling. "I guess so."

When someone dies, you know what to do. You know that there are plans to be made, there's a procedure, people to call and checks to write, and while you might be devastated, angry, confused, there is usually a plan to follow. And there are people to help you. Everyone will have to do this. Everyone will have to grieve. There is no handbook for how to be the family of a man who will go to prison for the rest of his life. There was no one to tell us how to grieve the loss of our brother who was still alive.

All of those things were being done for Christine. Her family was wearing black and making casseroles and writing the obituary. They didn't want any of us around; we couldn't go to the funeral. I understood, but also loved Christine. The grieving for her would have to come, someday, when it could rise to the surface and I could feel sad in appropriate ways.

Christine had worked in the hospital cafeteria. She had brown hair and green eyes and often got her nails done in neon colors or with designs, like zebra stripes or polka dots. When she was a kid, she thought she'd marry John Stamos. She was my friend.

"A spaghetti dinner," JD was saying. "And then a candlelight vigil. None of those people knew Christine." He was talking about one of the benefits that had sprung up over the past couple days. According to the flyers I'd seen in the Save-a-Lot, the proceeds would go to funeral expenses, and then the leftovers would be put in a fund in her name. The flyer didn't say what the fund was for, but different groups had gotten involved, like the rape and domestic violence organization, and Tanya said that probably there would be some kind of scholarship started for a graduating senior.

"Wonder if they'd give it to me," Andrea said. She'd meant it as a joke, but no one really laughed. School had been hard for both her and Matt. They'd only gone one day, and Matt had nearly gotten into a fistfight with a kid who'd coughed "murderer" as they'd passed in the hallway. Both had deleted their Facebook pages because of the nasty things that were being posted by people who hadn't known Christine or Jeff, but who believed any victim a martyr and any killer inherently evil.

"Adult people," Tanya said. "Grown-ups saying things like that to a teenager. And all these benefits. People who went to high school with Christine and haven't talked to her in twenty years, now crying on the news and releasing balloons in her memory. I sound like a bitch, but they don't know nothing about it."

"They just feel like they've got to do something," Jess said. He had spent some time inside with my parents, then came out and sat down on the ground next to me. He'd been holding a beer, but not drinking it. "They want to feel involved, I think. I guess most mean well."

"Bullshit," Robby said, drunker and drunker. "People need to get a goddamn life. Mind their own fucking business."

"Rob," JD said, and nodded toward the little ones, who were pretending not to listen, but I knew they really were. I had been that kid who'd always been around, playing with Barbies or scratching in the dirt when the grown-ups were talking. They'd always thought I was too little to understand.

It was full-on dark now and I had my head back as far as I could, looking at the stars. It was such a clear night, no clouds over the moon and the stars were as bright as I'd ever seen them.

"Mars," Jess said, and pointed to an orangish light. "It's kind of close to Earth right now, so you can see it good."

"Really? How'd you know that?" I asked.

Jess shrugged. "I read something about it in the newspaper yesterday. I like your new look, by the way," he teased. I glanced down at him and saw his eyes scanning my very exposed legs. Because of my collapsing chair, my knees were nearly level with my chin and from his angle, it probably looked as though I wasn't wearing any pants at all.

"Shut up," I said, and tilted my face back toward the sky. I felt his cool fingers come around my ankle, sending tiny cold electric charges up my leg.

"Maise," he said, softly, and I felt a question coming, something about how I was doing, or if I was okay. I was sick of those questions, and especially didn't want to hear one from Jess. I shook his hand away and started to struggle up from my chair.

"I'm going for a walk," I said. Jess was quickly to his feet and helped pull me up. "You can come on if you want to."

"It's dark," he said.

"Are you afraid?"

No one said anything when they saw us leave. I pretended like I didn't know where I was going, and first walked toward the barn. When we neared, Lily's lamb softly bleated for its mother, and I couldn't bear to go any closer. As a kid, I'd thought that sound was the saddest one in the world. It's what had made me bring a blanket out to the barn and sleep in the lamb's stall until my mother made me stop, what made me put a collar around its little black neck so that it could come with me when I worked in the garden or did my homework on the back porch. Daddy tried to tell me that animals didn't have feelings like that, and that I was being silly, but I never believed it.

Jess was softly humming "Mary had a little lamb." I thought at first that he was doing it to needle me, but when I turned, I saw that he was distracted, nervous, and probably didn't even realize he was humming at all.

"Come on," I said, and made a turn away from the barn.

"Maise, we shouldn't go over there," he said. He knew where we were going, even though I'd never said, and had probably known before we'd even left the fire.

"What? Where?"

"You know where. To Jeff's trailer. We shouldn't." Jess touched my wrist as if to stop me, but instead of stopping or pulling away, I let my fingers slip around his and pulled him with me. "Why do you want to do this to yourself?"

"I just need to see," I said, and when I said it I realized that it was true.

There was yellow police tape across the porch, hastily tied between banisters. I ducked under and pulled Jess with me. There was also tape stretched across the door in an X, and the similarities to TV shows made me laugh. "Someone's been watching too much CSI," I said and pulled the tape down by grabbing the X in the middle and ripping.

"Marianne, come on," Jess said, low like someone other than my drunk brothers and their wives might hear us. "You're going to get in trouble."

The door wasn't locked, thankfully. I hadn't even thought about that possibility until I turned the handle and it stuck a little, but then I pushed harder and it gave, opening up to the dark room.

"This is a bad idea," Jess said, but I knew he wouldn't try to stop me again, or make me go in alone.

"Find a light," I said, taking a couple tentative steps into the room. I'd been here before, of course, many times, but it had been a while. I was busy; I lived an hour away. Those were the excuses I made.

I took a few more steps in, heard Jess curse as he cracked his shin on an end table.

"I found the lamp," he said, then, "Maise, stop!" just as the light came on. I looked down and saw that I was just about to step onto a dark spot on the carpet. *Blood.* My brain said the word, but it somehow didn't register at first. I was seeing a stain, dark and purple, largish, but not big enough to be someone's poured-out life.

"Shit," Jess was near me again, and pulling me back. "We *should not* be in here."

What was I supposed to be feeling? Was I supposed to start crying? Screaming when I saw the place where Christine had died? I was only numb and tried to make myself feel more by picturing her lying there, Jeff standing over her, but it all seemed too unreal, and I could only think in clichés.

"She wanted to have kids," I said. "That's one thing they fought about. All these kids around and none of them hers. I guess that was hard for her." Jess slipped his hand back into mine. "I don't know why Jeff didn't want them. I should know that, shouldn't I?"

"Maybe," he said.

When we were married, Jess and I had fought. Really fought about money and jealousy, him holding me back and me pushing him to be something he wasn't. Without ever really saying the words, we fought about the baby I didn't have when I was eighteen. We were hard on each other, did everything full tilt, loving and fighting. I'd thrown things at him, scratched him, once bit him on the shoulder and drew blood. Once made him put our car into a ditch, and when people came out of their house to see if we were okay, he threatened them with a tire iron, and told them to get the hell away. He'd scream at me, threaten to hit, but never actually did. Once he pushed me and I fell back into our coal stove. I burned the back of my arm; he felt so bad that he cried. I slapped him hard across the face and wouldn't talk to him for three days. Too often we drank too much. We were too young. All the old excuses that boiled down to we fought against each other more than we fought to stay together, but we got away with only a few outside scars. But I knew how it felt to build up to losing control, for my brain and hands not to connect fast enough to stop from hitting, the blinding white light.

"Jess," I said, still staring hard at the dark spot on the carpet. "Did you ever think that we could have been here, if we hadn't have split?"

"Maise, no matter how mad I ever got, I never would have—"

I turned to him quickly, grabbed his face and kissed him hard, to stop him from saying anymore. I couldn't hear him tell me how he'd never hurt me, not when the picture I saw was him dying on the floor, me standing over him.

"Mais—" Jess tried to gently push me away, but I clung tight, as tight as I could. I'd needed to since he got down out of his truck. I knew always that he loved me still. "Stop," he said, but I could tell that he didn't mean it because he didn't move to leave.

"Why did you come tonight?" My fingers were wrapped up in his hair, my lips still nearly touching him. I was not letting him get away, would hurt him to stay. That is the feeling that had come over me. Only Jess knew who I really was and I had to have that honesty. He tried to pull away from me, but I held him tight. "Say it," I said. "Tell me."

"For you," he said, finally, looking me right in the eyes. "I came for you." He was kissing me, then, and holding me close to him. I was pulling at his shirt. "Not here," he said and pulled me out the door.

Around the side of the trailer, I took off the old sweatshirt and pulled Jess down onto the ground. I thought to laugh, the ridiculousness of this, rolling in the dirt like teenagers again, but Jess's eyes were dark, all serious, as he looked down at me and pulled off his own T-shirt. My fingers found the little white scar on his shoulder where my teeth had once broken his skin.

Gentle and careful were not something we ever were with each other. Jess's hands pushed my shoulders into the dirt; I felt the sharp rocks dig in. I hoped I bled.

It's funny how easy things come back, how easy the body remembers another body and things fall together just as they always had. It wasn't until after we were finished with each other, and Jess was sitting next to me with his head in his hands, that I remembered that the wedding ring on his left hand that had been pressing into my shoulder was not the one that I'd put on his finger. Jess had a new wife who was nice to him, and a little baby son. I remembered that Tanya had told me he'd stopped drinking. It occurred to me then why he'd just been holding that beer at the fire, the one that I couldn't remember if I had given him.

A part of me would never get over wanting him, to love him and to hurt him.

I pulled my shorts back on and found the sweatshirt. I was hot and gritty now, and when I pulled the shirt back on, it didn't feel cozy anymore, but smothering. "I'm going back," I said to Jess and started through the dark toward the fire.

They were quiet when I came back, and only Andrea looked up from the fire. The little ones were gone, to bed with my parents, and Robby was slumped over so that I couldn't tell if he was still awake. I sat back down beside Tanya and she patted my leg.

"He told me he wanted to die," JD said. He hadn't said much, but it was late enough, and he was drunk enough to talk. "When they let me in to see him after court today, he told me. He wants me to help him." No one said anything, just stared into the fire or at their own hands. "All day, I've been thinking, wondering if I should call the jail and tell them so that they could watch him better, you know? But I didn't call. And I've been thinking, god help me, I've been thinking all day how I could help him." JD sobbed, one then two loud, ugly gasps. Tanya went over to him, stood by him so that he could bury his face in her stomach.

I did not cry. Have not cried. Am not sure I remember how.

Jess came back and stood just outside of the circle, so that he was half in shadow, half in light. In my front sweatshirt pocket, my phone buzzed. It had somehow stayed there, safe, all along.

A text from Marcus: "Good night, sweetheart," it said, and "I'm sorry this is happening." Perfect punctuation. He said things in a text that he could not say in person.

I looked back up at Jess, through the swaying air around the flames and the smoke in my eyes. Beside him I saw Marcus in his white shirt and whimsical tie. And beside him, Jeff in orange, then Christine, looking like she had the last time I saw her, hair in a ponytail and wearing cutoff jean shorts. They were all looking at us, questioning, asking, "Of what are you capable?" My brothers, and me.

What Would Be Saved

———

Shed built a bonfire in the backyard. Books, picture albums, the never-used crib, bought on impulse when she first found out, now only an ugly wooden reminder, bare and empty with no sheep-covered comforter, with no powder-fresh baby.

First it had been matches, then a collection of cigarette lighters in a wooden box, some shaped like weapons and penises and some with flashing lights. Then there were candles on every table. She would tease the flames, show him how, if she moved quickly enough, she could put her hand right in and not get burned. After she went to sleep, he'd spend nearly an hour finding and blowing out all her small fires.

Today, this bonfire. When he came home, there was only thick smoke; a few small, glowing embers; the leg of a kitchen chair sticking out of the mess. She was wearing Bermuda shorts and a bikini top. In her hand was the garden hose, dripping.

"So," he said, standing in the doorway, drinking Dr Pepper from a can and looking aggressively calm. "What were you thinking?"

"I was thinking that a fire would be nice. It's a chilly day."

"I've definitely felt a briskness in the air," he said and held the chilly soda can to his forehead.

"I wanted to throw in the vanity," she said. "To be ironic, but I couldn't get it down the stairs. It's jammed in our bedroom doorway."

He noticed then that her face was dirty; he liked the clear lines that ran through the soot, down her cheeks, from eyes to chin. He pushed a thumb through the wetness.

"You're home early," she said.

Their nosy neighbor had called his office, concerned about his poor wife and their shared fence. *She may have gone crazy*, Mrs. Can't-Mind-Her-Own-Business said, sounding as though she'd been expecting something like this. She then reminded him of how damaging fire, when out of control, can be.

"Snow day," he said to his wife, who was not pitiful or crazy. Only burning up. Only trying to find a way to extinguish.

He looked at the smudge on his thumb and then tried to rub it off onto his own face, to unfreeze the frozen, like she wanted. There was only enough to make a small bruise under his eye. She took her own hand, sooty black and wet from the hose, and pressed a print across his cheek.

They marked one another in this prettier way. She drew a heart where his heart should be in thick ashes that had once been a picture of the cake cutting from their wedding day. He drew an empty circle on her belly with the remains of the crib. In the middle of her chest he tried to draw a question mark that wasn't really, so they went inside where they lay down on the kitchen floor to feel the coolness of the tile against skin on this hot, hot day.

Matches, lighters, candles, bonfire. One day it will be the house—every cobweb in corners and dust motes dancing in sunlight—any place where memories could cling. The only questions were the details. Accident or on purpose. Inside or out when the firemen came. What would be saved.

The Sound of Holding Your Breath

When Clint comes inside, I don't ask him where he's been. It's raining hard.

A giant puddle has formed in our front yard and some scrawny ducks have found it. I am watching them out the kitchen window as they glide around and dip their heads down into the big mud hole when the screen door thwacks shut behind me.

"Hello, honey," I say. I hope that he'll come up behind me, put his arms around my waist, and hug me close to him. The kitchen feels thick and heavy. I finger the tiny crucifix at my throat and say, "Still raining?"

"It is."

"I think it never will stop this time," I say, and a duck pops out of the puddle and ruffles his feathers. He shakes like a wet dog. "Better build an ark."

Clint takes his wet boots off by the door, like the good boy he is. I glance at him over my shoulder and see that he is shaking his head too, like the duck, like a dog, and little drops of water are flying around the kitchen. His hair is getting long. "You should let me cut that mop of yours tonight. It's starting to look pretty shaggy," I say, though I know he will not let me cut his hair. He is on pause, waiting. At first, I couldn't even get him to eat or drink anything. He wouldn't shower or change his clothes. He just watched out the back porch door and waited. I finally convinced him that he had to act more normal, and if the police came down our drive, he had to be like his old self, or we'd be done for.

I saw the lights early this morning, while he was still asleep. Our closest neighbor. It is too far away to see the cars, but in the dark early morning, I could see the red and the blue flashing up above the tree tops.

I waited an hour until the sun was higher and driving by on my way to town wouldn't look so suspicious. I left Clint a note: "Went in to the market. Don't go out there today."

I drove slow past Rob's place. It was like always, the house lopsided as if the right side was sinking into the ground, the white paint chipping off the porch, the old red truck and the nice little blue car parked out in front. There were two police cars in the driveway—one of the old white broncos that Sanders or Pete drove, and one of the newer, shinier blue cruisers from the sheriff's department. They were inside, so there was no way to tell the level of concern, who was taking what seriously. I imagined them sitting around the kitchen table, cups of weak coffee getting cold as Rob's wife Tiffany wiped mascara across her cheeks. His truck was in the driveway, but she hadn't seen him in about three days.

I imagined Tiffany pounding the table with her tiny little fists, crying harder as Pete or Sanders patted her shoulder, and the deputy, whichever one had been unlucky enough to be sent all the way out to our skinny dirt roads, squirmed uncomfortably. Crystal didn't understand— she never could—because she came here already grown. You have to be here from the start, born out into the dirt and the woods and the mountains and the close inside feeling—like me, like Clint, like Rob— to really know.

Some days I feel off my axis, wobbly or spinning, but today I feel sharp and clear.

I don't know how to explain the quiet here, except to say that there are chirping birds and leaves rustling, but the loudest sound is the nothingness. The house has been in Clint's family for generations. It is tall and has those windows in the front that look like eyes, always watching me, like it just took a big breath and is waiting to breathe out, if only I'd get out of the way. Maybe that's the way to describe the quiet: it's the sound of holding your breath.

The quiet is a little less when Clint is here.

This morning when I got home and Clint was gone, the house stared at me in the breath-holding way. I went inside, slammed the kitchen door, and almost immediately the sky grew dark and the rain came, hard like bullets.

Rob James grew up in that lopsided house out the road. His daddy worked a dirt farm for most of his life, worked himself to death to try to raise a little corn, a little patch of beans, and tomatoes. Baking his brain in the hot summer sun to cut the hay for his few skinny cows. He died on that tractor the summer I was thirteen. Rob was friends with my older brother Patrick, and his daddy paid Pat a dollar a day to help in the hayfields.

Rob's dad died on that tractor. He always drove in perfect lines. Pat said that the way they first knew something was wrong was because the tractor started going off course, left to the tree line instead of straight ahead. They were shouting at him, then running because they saw that he had slumped over in his seat. Finally, he fell out and they all watched as the big back tire of the tractor rolled over his body. At least the baler missed him.

Rob was over at our house a lot that summer. He and Pat would walk down to the creek out back to fish or catch crawdads. I'd follow along when they let me, or when they didn't see me. Sometimes Rob's older brother would drive us all to Flat Rocks, a popular swimming hole where the water ran over smooth rocks, creating perfect natural water slides. I was never graceful like my brother or the other boys—I was always a little too fat, a little too clumsy—and would end up falling before I was ready, slipping and bruising a knee or elbow.

The water collected in a whirling pool at the bottom, and our bodies would bash together. The boys would push each other under. I'd bob around and splash, until I felt a hand on my ankle, knee, thigh, then I'd scream and kick. I was the only girl, but I didn't feel different. I was included, and that's all I ever wanted. When Rob would snap the strap of my swimsuit, I'd squeal and try to punch him.

That year Pat had a job bagging groceries at the market, and Mom and Dad worked until six. I don't know how Rob knew I'd be there alone, but I guess when you live in a place like this, everybody knows everything. The first time he showed up, he said he was looking for Pat. He was sixteen then and his mom let him drive the farm-use truck. He didn't come every day, but just about, and if I ever told him to leave, I can't remember.

Rob started asking if I wanted to go swimming, and he'd tell me to put on my bathing suit, but then we wouldn't go. He'd look at me and say something like, "When you gonna lose that baby fat, Marley?" He'd want to watch TV or play Monopoly. He'd sit on his side of the table, and I'd sit on mine, but he'd tell me not to waste time changing my clothes. Then, sometimes when we were watching TV, he'd put his hand on my knee or my thigh.

When he started asking me if I wanted to go back into my bedroom, I'm sure I said no. I didn't cry, but once I bit the inside of my lip so hard it bled into my mouth. I think I said no.

Good and bad can be so close together. We all are always brushing up against the line. Evil doesn't exist. The evil thing is just the quick other side of the beautiful thing. It's the mouth full of blood next to the boy's hand moving higher.

I never told. I bled and cried; Rob threw up and swore never to come back, but he did, and then hated himself again. When Pat got fired from the market and started coming home with me after school, Rob was released from his own horrible self, and never spoke to me again.

No one ever knew but me and Rob, and it was the slimy gray thread that kept us always attached. We circled each other, but never spoke, never touched. I always knew what he was doing, though. I always caught him out of the corner of my eye. When he got arrested for driving drunk, I knew, and later when it was the pills, I knew that too. Even that one year when I went away, thinking that I could be a college girl, I kept up with Rob through my parents or Pat.

Then I came home, and there was Clint, the same fair-haired boy I'd always known. He'd always been there, just on the outskirts of my gaze. Once I learned how to focus, it all made sense. We got married, and we moved into his parents' house. They moved to town, but still show up unexpectedly to mow the grass or mop the kitchen.

Every day I passed the lopsided house. Sometimes I saw Rob out in his yard. I'd slow my car down, and we'd lock eyes, then he'd duck his head and shuffle off.

Clint is sweet. He has little ambition beyond keeping the house in order, making enough money at his job with the state road to feed us and keep us warm. He wants a baby and I don't mind the idea. We've been trying for over a year and every time we fail, I feel Clint getting a little smaller.

One day earlier this year, Rob's old truck was not alone in his driveway. There was this little shiny blue car, and Clint joked about how that thing was never going to move once the snow started. Something had changed.

I asked around, and I found out there was a woman behind the little blue car, a woman with the ridiculous name of Tiffany who was from somewhere else—Columbus or Dayton—someplace flat. I asked my mom how they met, and she said that some people were saying on the internet.

"I bet she sure was shocked when she got here," I said, but Mom just shrugged her shoulders.

"People in town say she seems real nice and is pretty. And you know, I ain't heard anybody say a thing about Rob causing trouble down at the Golden Egg for a while now. I guess maybe he's turning it around."

Then the little blue car showed up in my driveway, and out of it stepped a blonde woman-child wearing high-heeled boots that sank into the mud. I wanted to laugh as I watched her struggle from the kitchen window, but somehow instead of her looking silly, her sinking boot just made us look poor.

She walked around the car—her heel sticking just about every other step—opened the passenger-side door, and took out a domed cake plate.

When she knocked, instead of moving over to answer the door, I slumped down against the bottom cupboard. I pulled my knees up to my chest and waited as she knock, knock, knocked. Called "Hullo?" in her high sugar voice.

She finally gave up, and I heard the car drive away, but I waited a few minutes anyway, just to be safe, before getting up from my hiding spot.

She'd left the cake plate on the welcome mat, along with a note that said "Happy to Meet You!" in pretty, curling letters. The cake was not so pretty, uneven and frosted with some toxic pink buttercream.

Later, I scraped the whole thing into the trash.

According to my mother, Tiffany spent a lot of time in town. She shopped and went to the library. She was going to volunteer for the blood drive. She was charming everyone right out of their pants with her can-do attitude. Every time she came to my door knock, knock, knocking, I hid in a dark corner or in an upstairs bedroom until she left. The cake plate sat unwashed on my counter.

She came up on my porch three, maybe four times. Once, I was upstairs and could watch her from above as she tried to peek in our windows to see if anyone was home. I thought about spitting on her head, or maybe dropping something heavy—just to scare her off.

Finally, it was Rob's old red truck that came bouncing toward the house. He sat in the truck for a long time before opening the door, but then his steps were quick. He stomped up the driveway and was on the porch, pounding on the door so hard it liked to shake the entire house.

"Marley, come open the goddamn door," he said. "I come for Mama's cake plate."

I should have slumped back into the kitchen corner. Or opened the window over the sink and tossed the cake plate as far as I could. Instead, though, I patted down my hair, picked up the cake plate, and calmly walked to the door.

I opened it just as Rob lifted his fist to pound again, stopping just before punching me in the face. I flinched but didn't jump back.

"I come for Mama's cake plate," he said again. It had been a long time since I'd really seen him up close. His dark hair was cut close to his head, but I could tell that it was starting to thin. His face was skinny and the skin looked stretched tight, tiny lines around his eyes and mouth. Nose, cheek bones, chin—all sharp angles.

"You didn't have to try and bust the door down," I said. My voice cracked and I felt as though these were the first words I'd said in a long time, in years maybe.

"I wanted to make sure you heard me since you didn't seem to ever hear Tiffany when she came by."

"Maybe I wasn't here," I said and took a step out the door. Rob took a step back.

"I 'spect you were, in there hiding like some little kid."

"Why would I do that? Do you think I'm afraid of your little girlfriend? I never asked her to come out here in the first place, you know."

"Wife," Rob said, almost spitting the word at me. He took a step forward, and I did not back up. "Tiffany is my wife, and I got sick of seeing her come home sad because some stuck-up bitch out the road wouldn't answer the door when all she was trying to be was nice."

I felt slapped. Being called stuck up was about the worst thing you could be called. It meant you were full of pride, felt better than your neighbors, above your raising.

"You best watch what you say to me, Rob James. Don't push me too far."

"That supposed to be some sort of threat? You don't even know me,

Marley," Rob laughed, a mean little laugh just to show how unafraid he was still, after all these years. It was like no time had passed, really.

"I sure knew you once," I said, my voice low. All the parts of me were colliding—I couldn't stop them. I was anger and wickedness; fear and open, pulsating need.

"Christ Almighty!" Rob said. "That was a hundred years ago. We was just kids."

"*I* was just a kid," I said. "And if I told wifey the next time she comes snooping around, I bet that's how she'd see it, too."

Before I had time to think, Rob had grabbed me hard by the shoulders and pushed me up against the wall. In his eyes was a darkness I remembered, and I knew he wasn't so different, wasn't so changed from the boy who'd told me to put on my swimsuit, who'd left finger-shaped bruises on my pale, fleshy thigh.

"You always were crazy," Rob said, his face so close now that I felt his moist breath on my lips. His grip on my arms hurt and I tried to push him away, but he held me fast, shook me a little so that my head bounced off the wall. "Watching me, asking about me. You think I didn't know? I always knew what you were up to."

"Let me go," I said.

"I love my wife," Rob said, now nearly breathing into my mouth. "You leave us both be. You hear me?"

"You did this," I said, pushing my face so close to his that our lips nearly touched. "You connected us. Can't undo it now." I latched on to his lip, biting him hard. I tasted the blood again, his blood filling my mouth, his rubbery flesh between my teeth.

Rob screamed, the sound muffled from my bite, and released me. He lifted his arm and slammed me across the left side of my head. I fell hard on the splintered porch floor, my ear ringing and on fire.

"You crazy bitch," Rob said, and spat his own mouthful of blood. He took a step toward me, but I did not back up. I did not slink away. Then Rob was the one moving through the air, his eyes wide as

Clint pulled him backward by his collar. Rob was tall, but skinny and no match for Clint's strong arms.

"What the hell?" Clint said as Rob whirled around to face him.

"Whoa," Rob said and put his hands up. Then I started to scream. I don't remember what I said. It could have been something about Rob, about touching my thigh, holding me down, swimsuits. It could have been about twenty years ago, but Clint only heard today.

I screamed and screamed. I couldn't stop screaming.

I do believe that we were put on the road to this moment a long time ago, and there was nothing that could have stopped it from happening. Ever since that day at Flat Rocks when a boy touched me under the water and could not stop touching me. Every day had been leading to this. It had to be so.

How else could you explain the push, nothing more than a hard tap on Rob's shoulders, that sent him off the edge of the porch? His arms windmilled. He disappeared.

Clint stood on the edge, staring down. I finally stood and came up behind my husband, who could already tell the truth.

People survive amazing accidents all the time. They fall from silos, get thrown through windshields. They get shot and stabbed and nearly drowned, but they live. Rob fell from our front porch and landed just right, his head bashing against one of Clint's mother's ugly lawn statues: a little stone girl holding a watering can.

Rob was not moving, and he was not just knocked out cold. His eyes were staring upward. There was blood on the little girl. "Shit," I said.

"I'll call 911," Clint said and started toward the door, but I stopped him.

"You can't."

"Christ, Marley. I got to."

"Why? What's done is done and you getting locked up isn't going to help any of that."

"But I had to," Clint stammered. "They'll see. He was hurting you." I shook my head and put my hands on Clint's face. He was crying. He was a little boy. I kissed him, forgetting that I had Rob's blood still on my mouth.

"You can't, Clint. They won't understand." Clint was shaking, crying harder and harder. I never could stand to see a man cry, so I pulled his head down to my shoulder. "We'll take care of this," I said. "It will be okay."

The only way to go about it was to pretend it was a movie, and we were actors playing a role that someone else wrote for us.

I drove past Rob's house first, to make sure the little blue car was gone. Tiffany was volunteering at the library, like she did every other weekday until five. I pulled in the driveway and called Clint, who came shortly in Rob's truck. I made sure that he parked it just how Rob would have. I put the cake plate on the kitchen counter and left the truck keys lying right next to it.

When we got home, I cleaned the blood off the stone girl.

He'd handled Rob's body all himself—wouldn't even let me see where he'd dug the hole—and I'm proud of him for that. He said that he dug out the space under one of the big, flat rocks that jutted out, and I hoped it was the one that the big sugar maple grew next to. It was smart to dig under that rock, and then put Clint in deep. It'd be nearly impossible to see there, and Clint said that after he'd packed the dirt back in, he'd scattered around leaves and twigs and made it look as normal as he could. Now, if he'd just stay away.

Every day he goes out there, disappears for hours, and when he comes home he reeks of woods and doubt and regret. He has not been back to work, and if he doesn't go in tomorrow, people will start to ask questions. That's why tonight I am going to tell him about the baby.

I imagine it, a wiggly little tadpole thing in my belly. It's not there yet, but it will be. It was all supposed to happen just this way, and now the baby will come and it will bring Clint back. He will resurface, like a soldier coming home from war, and accept that he has done things that were ugly but necessary.

When did I see Clint first? Was it before I bit Rob's lip or after?

Tiffany will have to go back to Ohio. When she came up my drive that first time, I saw her shirt starting to stretch around the little bump of her belly. If the little blue car comes up my drive again, this time I'll make friends, and convince her that this is no place for a city girl, alone with a baby. If you aren't from here, you just can't understand.

I hear Clint stomping back down the stairs. He has changed out of his wet clothes and is wearing new ones that look almost just the same— black T-shirt, jeans. His socks are gone, and something about his bare white feet is so tender, so vulnerable, that I want to hug him tight. I only want to keep him safe, inside.

"Them ducks still out there?" he asks me.

"Sure are," I say, and rub my belly, trying again to conjure that picture of a little Clint, a little Marley, baby-worm.

"You were out in the woods again." I don't ask, and Clint doesn't answer. "You have to stop, honey."

"I can't just let it go," he says.

"You have to," I say, and take a deep breath. "You have to, for the sake of the baby."

I feel Clint breathe in behind me. Then, his arms encircle me, his hands spread out over my belly. Familiar and good. All right. He kisses my neck, and then leaves his head there.

I want the rain to stop, for a rainbow to stretch across the sky, but it does not. The sky is gray, the puddle grows. A duck's head disappears again, and I hold my breath until he resurfaces, shaking, enjoying the storm.

Stalking the White Deer

———

Dalton stalked the white deer. It became his obsession, like finding that thing and owning it in a hard, bloody way would fill a hole neither of us could name. We were newly married then and him just back from the war. He'd been home about a year, but it always seemed like he was just back. For years. Even now. It was always lingering there, but our boys came back into their lives, all messed up—in body and in spirit—and went right back to it. Bury it in the mines. Cut it down with the trees. Drive, drink, drug, and screw it away. But don't name it.

I told him to leave the white deer be and he laughed at me. "Jezzie, girl, did you get all soft on me while I was gone? Do you want to make a pet out of that deer?" Some men liked gentle and sweet women, but Crystal men wanted girls who could never be called delicate. Maybe it had to be that way because of the kind of life we live. Some fragile little thing would never survive it, would end up in a crazy house or in the ground.

First Dalton only wanted the white deer—he'd seen it once, out behind his daddy's house, and it had been so shocking that he'd blinked a few times to make sure that he wasn't looking at a dog or a ghost. "When it ran away," he told me, "it was like smoke or mist moving through the trees." He wanted it so bad that he wouldn't take any others, and I started to worry that we'd have no deer meat to put up for the winter. I didn't have long to worry, though, because then Dalton got bad and started killing all those deer just out of rage. Our little yard was full of deer, hanging from trees, dripping blood. He killed them faster than we could butcher them. They started rotting, and the smell turned to something different than just death.

Dalton stayed out every hour he could, roaming along the ridges with his gun, searching for that white deer.

My belly was big then. We thought there would be just one baby, but when I grew and grew, we went to the doctor over in Oakland and he said that there'd be two. I thought about what my granny used to tell me about twins, how the old folks thought it wasn't natural, and how some wouldn't let both babies live. "I ain't saying that's right," Granny said, "but I ain't never seen a set where both turn out good." Granny was old then, and her face was shriveled like a dried-up apple, but she had these blue eyes that seemed almost to glow. I was only a girl, fourteen or fifteen, and she just stared right into me, like she knew one day I'd be sitting in this drafty old house, full to the brim with babies, dead animals rotting all around me.

When Dalton came in from the woods, he'd go back to the bedroom and strip off all his clothes, covered in blood and other dark stains that I couldn't think about. He'd shower quick and then come out into the kitchen, where I'd have his dinner—little that it was—waiting. He wouldn't put clothes back on, and I never could get used to seeing him walk around in the kitchen, pale and skinny, without a stitch on. It embarrassed me and I couldn't look at him straight on, like some little girl seeing a man for the first time. Sometimes, he'd think it was funny, and laugh that mean little laugh he had, then press up against me, just to feel me try to squirm away. Other times he'd look at me with disgust. "You act like the Virgin Mary," he'd say and sneer. "Well them ain't God's babies rolling around inside you."

"That's ugly talk," I'd say. He'd shrug and sit at the table, eat his dinner with that blood and mud deep under his fingernails and in the creases of his knuckles.

Rabbits, groundhogs, raccoons, lying all around our little house. Then that red fox. It had started to snow and his bright coat stood out among all the others. I saw it from the kitchen window and had to go out, a part of me maybe hoping it was still alive and that Dalton wouldn't have killed such a beautiful thing just because he could, just because he couldn't have what he really wanted. His work coat was hanging by the door, and I wrapped it around me. I was so big then with the babies that it would barely stretch across. I liked the smell of it that reminded me of Dalton—the woods and the grease from the coal trucks he worked on for Shaffer Trucking.

More and more he'd been missing work, taking off all or part of the day to roam the ridges. They'd been understanding and old man Shaffer had grown up with Dalton's daddy, but I knew one day they'd have had enough and Dalton would have no job. Some nights, I'd look at his face as he leaned over his dinner plate, and I'd get so afraid of what I saw there. He could lose his job and not care a bit. Me and him and the babies could starve to death or freeze to death in the coldest days of winter, and still he would not care.

Dalton had tossed the fox next to the woodpile, already at its lowest since we'd lived there. His eyes were open and as I got closer, I thought maybe he was still breathing. I am ashamed to say that then I started hoping and hoping that it was not so. I did not know how to take care of an injured fox. I did not want to try. The beautiful thing was dead, though, the tip of his tongue out the side of his mouth, the white scruff of his neck brown with dried blood.

Dalton was standing in our little kitchen when I came back inside. He had spent all morning since before dawn stalking that white deer, but must have come in from the ridge while I was out back with the fox. My stomach clenched, thinking about what new dead thing he'd soon have strung up in our trees, but then I saw that his hands were clean, and so were his clothes. Nothing this morning.

"What were you doing, Jezzie?" he asked.

"I just went out to check the woodpile," I lied. "It's getting low." He came toward me then and though he'd never hit me, someplace inside I always knew that he could, that all men could. I took a step back, my hand stretching for the door handle, but when Dalton reached me, he wasn't angry.

He put his big hands on my cheeks and said, "Cold?" I nodded. He said, "Come over to the fire. Your feet—" My feet had been too swollen for weeks to put on my boots so I'd gone out in my house slippers. The snow had collected around the tops. I hadn't even noticed.

Dalton led me to the big chair next to the fire and kneeled down in front of me. "What were you thinking, Jezzie girl? Your feet are like ice." He pulled the slippers off and rubbed my freezing feet, blowing hot breath on my toes, and then kneading my skin with his strong hands.

"He is pushing life back into me," I thought, as the burning pain of feeling poured into my feet.

"I'm sorry, Jezzie," he said, so low I could barely hear him. When he gently kissed the top of my burning foot, a jolt shot through me that nearly made me laugh and cry all at the same time. "I'll go cut more wood for the pile. Don't you worry about that."

"I ain't worried," I said. I wanted to reach down and cup his face in my hands, but my big belly stopped me.

"I'll go right now," he said, but instead kissed my ankle.

"No, don't go," I said, and stretched my hand out for him, though he was just out of my reach. Dalton rubbed my calf and kissed my knee, pushing my housedress up over my thighs. A young woman still and here I was wearing a housedress and slippers like a granny. Dalton kissed the inside of my thigh and I thought about the boy he had been, the towheaded kid who sat behind me every year in school because my last name started with a *b* and his started with a *c*. The boy with a daddy so mean he'd sometimes cut Dalton's hair in an awful way to punish him for not doing something fast enough. He'd come to school with chunks taken out of the side—his scalp raw and pink underneath. I suppose his daddy was hoping to humiliate him, but the other kids were too scared of the Crystals to ever make fun.

Once, he'd saved a kitten whose mother got ran over on the county road. The kitten was so tiny, and he fed it with an eyedropper until it got big enough to eat on its own.

Once, he gave me his lunch money because I didn't have any.

Once, he took my hand and led me out to the cemetery and showed me where all the generations of Crystals were buried. "We're all here," he'd said. "Planted right here in this ground while we're living and while we're dead." I knew he was telling me that he could never leave Warm, and if I wanted to be with him, I could never leave either.

He kissed the inside of my thigh and I remembered the girl I was, not some scared little mouse, shivering in a corner. I was a strong girl who chopped wood all those months Dalton was away, who worked at the five-and-ten in town and who hadn't been scared of much of anything.

"He is pushing life back into me," I thought again as he put his hands on either side of my belly. "I will do the same for him."

"Don't cut that wood," he said into my ear the next morning before leaving for work.

"I won't," I mumbled, and he kissed my temple.

"I mean it," he said. "Don't chop the wood. I'll do it when I get home."

He was the old Dalton, the Dalton before he left for the war and forgot how to stop killing, but I knew it wouldn't last. I'd seen it before—a day or two or even three of the boy I knew, but then the dark would come back into his face and he'd see things in his head again that I couldn't understand.

I put on my heaviest sweater and found a pair of Dalton's pants in the closet. Nothing I had fit me anymore—only those old housedresses, and I knew this was not a job I could do in a dress. I put on three pairs of socks, then shoved my feet down into his old boots. They were still too big but would have to do. I smiled to see that he'd left his work coat hanging on a hook by the door for me.

If I'd had a brother, my daddy's rifle would have gone to him, but since I didn't, it had been mine after he'd died. I kept it clean and oiled, but I hadn't shot it in years. I knew how, though, and that was one of those things that once you learned, you never did forget. When I put the butt up to my shoulder and looked through the sights, my finger curled around the trigger just like it had been waiting to do for so long.

I thought about going back to Dalton's daddy's house where he'd first spotted the white deer, but that seemed too dangerous. His daddy or one of his brothers might see me. So I just started walking out of Crystal Holler, up Backbone Mountain. It was cold enough to see my breath, but not as cold as the day before. There was a dusting of new snow. If I got close to any animal, it'd be easy enough to see its tracks.

I can't explain how I knew where to go. I thought maybe God had led me there to find that white deer, to take her life and save my own. But now, as an old woman who has seen a life of one hard, heartbreaking thing after another, I can say that if there is a God, he is a son of a bitch, and if that day in the woods was a test, I failed it.

I'd been out for only an hour or so, trying to keep quiet as I could. I slipped once and went down to one knee. I'm ashamed to say that I did not stop then to think about my babies and what would happen to them if I tumbled down the steep hillside. Throughout my life, I have always thought more about my husband than those boys, and that is my great shame. That is what happens, though, when you love a boy from the time you were both children, when you can't stand to love anything more.

She stepped right out in front of me, maybe a hundred yards or so ahead of where I had stopped to catch my breath. It was just like Dalton had said, a ghost deer so white I wasn't sure she was real. She stopped when she saw me and just stood there, staring, steam from her nose floating out around her head.

What I should say is that she was so beautiful that I didn't want to kill her. The truth, though, is that as I raised the rifle to my shoulder and put the crosshairs on the white deer's neck, I could already see the red rose blooming through her coat, her falling to the ground.

"Good girl," I thought, but did not say. I did not want to spook her. I was a good shot, and I knew where I should hit the deer to make it all quick and easy. I did not want to chase her through the woods, injured and frantic. I did not want her to suffer. A good hunter knows not to take a life for granted.

My finger squeezed the trigger and I barely felt the kick against my shoulder. Just as I imagined, the deer jerked and then fell. The blood, though, was not a bright red like I'd pictured. As I walked to her, I saw that it was dark, nearly black, and spread over her neck not like a rose, but like an ugly stain, spilled paint. She was not breathing or moving, and that at least was something.

I had not thought about what would happen next, how I would get the white deer down from the ridge, or if I should slit her belly there like I knew the men did. If you let it go too long, if you didn't stick them and bleed them, the meat will turn bad. I could not imagine eating the meat of the white deer or frying it in a pan. I gagged at the thought.

I heard a rustling over in the bramble, and then a crying sound, a scream almost. A sickness came over me as the knowing set in. There shouldn't have been a baby now, not at this time of the year, but there it was, spindly legged and spotted. I now knew why she hadn't run from me, smart girl protecting her little one.

"Oh, I'm sorry," I said to the fawn. "I'm sorry, baby."

"Jezzie?" I started. In my craziness—my exhaustion—I thought the deer was saying my name. "What are you doing? What—"

Through the woods behind me came Dalton, carrying his own rifle. He hadn't gone to work like he'd said, but was up on the ridge, just like me. He looked from me to the white deer, and then to the bleating fawn in the brush. "Jesus Christ," he said. "What are you doing?"

"I just wanted to help you," I said. I made to touch his arm, but he pushed me away.

"Have you lost your fucking mind?"

"Dalton—"

"Go home," he said, staring down at the white deer.

"I can help. We can drag her out of here, and then this can be over," I said. I saw him look over at the fawn, still standing uncertainly in the brambles, wanting to go to its mother.

"Go home," Dalton said again. "Go now."

Only more harm would come if I tried to argue, so I turned and started carefully away from my kill. I wanted to believe that maybe Dalton would save that fawn, coax it over to him and wrap it up in his big arms, nurse it with a baby bottle like he did that kitten when he was a boy. If he had done that, then I would have known this all could still be set right, and that our lives could take on a different shape— maybe a rose shape again, but I had only taken a few steps when I heard the crack of the rifle. For a crazy minute, I thought maybe Dalton had put the barrel of the rifle under his own chin. Lord knows it wouldn't have been the first time someone from around here'd had a hunting accident like that, but when I turned, I saw his back, shoulders slumped forward, crying.

Some folks think it's cowardly to kill a white deer because they're so easy to see with no natural camouflage. Others say it's bad luck. I don't believe in luck, but I do know this: when Dalton came down from the ridge that day, he did not bring the white deer or the fawn. He did borrow his father's tractor and dig a big hole. He spent two days hauling the dead animals into that hole, as I watched from the kitchen window. I couldn't get the sound of that baby crying out of my head or stop picturing the way Dalton's shoulders shook after he killed it. Those were my burdens to carry, though, and I'd do it gladly if it meant my husband was fixed. What I did not know then, could not know, was that a human cannot be fixed. They can be patched, and soothed, and made to remember a little less, but fixed is something Dalton would never be.

When my babies came, they came early. Dalton drove me to the hospital in Oakland, his knuckles white where they clutched the steering wheel, and his lips a tight, thin line. He did not speak to me the whole drive and stared only straight ahead.

Walker came into the world a screaming fireball, but Sam was born quiet and with the caul covering his face. My granny would have shaken her head with worry, but she was long dead. The doctor said what good luck it was, and rare, to see a baby born that way. The doctor said Sam would be blessed his whole life. I wondered what that meant for Walker, the baby who always cried.

I watched my boys grow, loved them the best I could, and I truly think Dalton did the same, in the only ways he knew how. Sometimes that was a backhand to the mouth, other times it was an arm across the shoulder. He helped them with the hard things, like burying their dog when it got run over by the mailman, then burying their grandfather when an aneurysm burst in his brain. I cooked them dinner, and washed their clothes, and gave them dollars at the end of every week, even when there weren't many dollars to go around. I tried to help them be good boys—the both of them—and I tried not to notice the shining light around Sam, or the dark shadow around his brother. Sometimes I'd remember that white deer and the baby, screaming in the brush, and I'd punish myself by thinking, "Which one, Jezzie? If you could save just one baby, which one would it be?" On my most honest days, I knew it would be Sam, so I showered Walker with love. I made him special things for dinner and snuck him an extra quarter or two when I could. Sam pretended never to notice or to care, because he was good in a way none of the rest of us was. He was a smart boy, and sweet. They both were so handsome. But they were Crystals, and even the good Crystals have a dark side that craves booze and drugs and driving fast and living hard. I knew this, always, and I chose it. Is killing the white deer what cursed my boys or was it marrying Dalton Crystal?

When Walker and Sam were fifteen, Dalton took them to the family cemetery and said to them, "This is your kin, boys, all of it. We're all planted right here in this ground while we're living and while we're dead." He was asking them to make the decision, just as he had me all those years ago. Are you going to be one of us?

Dalton and me, we are here, together, for better or worse in the life we deserve. If I had it to do over again, even after all that has happened, I suspect I would do it just the same way. When people look at us, living here in this holler with not much money or anything else, and say, "What's wrong with you?" I guess that's the answer. We stayed, we stay, we always will. Through ugliness, and blood, one boy dead and one tattered, we are our stain, the stain that we made.

Acknowledgments

I must first thank West Virginia University Press and my wonderful editor, Abby Freeland. I owe her, Derek Krissoff, Sara Georgi, Rachel King, Than Saffel, and everyone at the press an unpayable debt of gratitude. I also am very thankful to all of the literary journals that have previously published my work.

Thank you to Copper Canyon Press for granting me permission to use several lines from C. D. Wright's poem "Everything Good Between Men and Women," which appear as the epigraph for this volume.

I must also acknowledge the support, time, and community given to me by a number of fabulous organizations, including the Mid Atlantic Arts Foundation, the West Virginia Humanities Council, Virginia Center for the Creative Arts, Hindman Settlement School and the Troublesome Creek Writers' Retreats, the Kentucky Women Writers Conference, and the West Virginia Writers' Workshop. I'm also proud to be a part of the Women of Appalachia Project.

I thank the Appalachian Heritage Writer-in-Residence program, the *Anthology of Appalachian Writers*, and especially Dr. Sylvia Bailey Shurbutt for inviting me to be an editor and a board member. Meeting the writers who have come to Shepherdstown each year has been invaluable to me.

Throughout my life I have loved books in all forms and have been lucky enough to have had the ability to surround myself with words. This started when I was a baby and my mother read to me every night. When I was five, Joel Bean at the Kingwood Public Library gave me my first library card. Mrs. McLoughlin saw my potential to be a writer when I was in the sixth grade and urged me to write for more than just class assignments. Mrs. Jenkins gave me *The Diary of Anne Frank* and taught me how to diagram a sentence. Thank you to all the teachers and librarians who have encouraged me.

When I was a freshman in college, I walked into a creative writing class, thinking that it would be my elective and nothing more. I met Gail Adams, and everything changed. Thank you, Gail, for being my teacher, mentor, and especially my friend.

I have also been honored to find myself part of a circle of strong and supportive Appalachian writers who have given me advice as well as fellowship. To name just a few, thank you: Silas House, Jason Howard, Marianne Worthington, Marc Harshman, Gretchen Moran Laskas, Doug Van Gundy, Wiley Cash, Randi Ward, Robert Gipe, and—of course—the fabulous Ann Pancake. Thank you especially Laura Long for your belief in me, your guidance, and your encouragement. Without you, this collection would not exist.

Thank you Jill for being my friend and having dinner with me when I really need it; thank you Renee for always being my partner in literary crime; and thank you Melissa for being there for me, reading anything I ever asked you to, listening to all my freak-outs, and designing an awesome website for me. What would I do without you all?

Finally, I must thank my family who always let me be just who I am. My parents lived with me and my books and my papers, and only complained occasionally. My grandparents told me stories since birth and inspire me in everything I do. Brie is good-hearted and quirky, and destined for amazing things. Felina, Daisy, and Fern are just the hounds a writer needs.

Thank you. Thank you all.

Reading and Discussion Questions

———

1. What common themes and connecting threads do you see in this collection?

2. Many of the stories deal with the theme of identity—the search for it, or the desire to escape it. How do you see the theme of identity working in this collection?

3. Several of these stories are narrated by young adults. Do you find the young narrators reliable? More or less so than the adult narrators? Why?

4. Several of these stories include seemingly good characters who do bad or evil things (like killing a neighbor, for instance). Can good people commit evil deeds, or does the ability to commit the deed mean they were never good in the first place?

5. Why do you think Jenny decided to serve Matt the bloody-knuckle salad in "Lettuce"?

6. In the title story, what responsibility do you feel Marley holds in Rob's death?

7. Which characters do you feel most connected to and why?

8. While these stories are clearly set in Appalachia, they are not necessarily traditional Appalachian stories. What elements of Appalachian literature do you see present? How do these stories deviate from the traditional?

9. What do you believe these stories demonstrate about West Virginia and West Virginians?

10. "How far would you go?" is a question many of these stories ask. How far would you go for love? For protection? For the life you want to have?

CPSIA information can be obtained
at www.ICGtesting.com
Printed in the USA
BVHW07s2120220918
528133BV00005BB/9/P